# The Cora Tree Murder
## An Outer Banks Mystery

A novel by

**Joe C. Ellis**

# What Readers Are Saying:

"This was the best book of the Outer Banks mystery series. It blends relationships with suspense, intrigue, a bit of whimsy, and of course...murder. I couldn't put it down."
Chuck S.

"The twists and turns add to the excitement of the story. I can't wait for Joe's next story to be released."
Milton W.

"I thoroughly enjoyed this story by author, Joe Ellis. Having spent many days on the Outer Banks and learning the legends and tales of the area, Mr. Ellis tells a superb story. He includes Angie Stallone once again with the help of locals to solve the mystery. I love not only how he includes some of the island's shops, restaurants and points of interest, but how he intertwines all of them in an old legend and comes up with a thrilling story. When I read this book, it takes me to the Outer Banks of North Carolina."
Jim A.

"I have enjoyed the Outer Banks Mystery Series, and I think that this one is my favorite! I loved the characters and the storyline. This series makes me want to visit the Outer Banks even more! Can't wait for the next book!"
Jana S.

"A must read! Highly recommended, especially for those that love murder mysteries and the Outer Banks."
Ganne B.

Upper Ohio Valley Books
Joe C. Ellis
71299 Skyview Drive
Martins Ferry, Ohio 43935
Email: **joecellis@comcast.net**

PUBLISHER'S NOTE

Although this novel, *The Cora Tree Murder*, is set in actual locations on the Outer Banks of North Carolina, it is a work of fiction. The characters' names are the products of the author's imagination. Any resemblance of these characters to real people is entirely coincidental. Many of the places mentioned in the novel—Buxton Village Books, Historic Cottage Row, the Cape Hatteras Lighthouse, Billy Mitchell Aerodrome, Conner's Market in Buxton, Rusty's Surf and Turf and other places mentioned in the novel—are real locations. However, their involvement in the plot of the story is purely fictional. It is the author's hope that this novel generates great interest in this wonderful region of the U.S.A., and, as a result, many people will plan a vacation at these locations and experience the beauty of these settings firsthand.

CATALOGING INFORMATION
Ellis, Joe C., 1956-
**The Cora Tree Murder**
*An Outer Banks Mystery*
by Joe C. Ellis

1.Outer Banks—Fiction. 2. Buxton—Fiction
3. Mystery—Fiction 4. Suspense—Fiction
5. North Carolina—Fiction 6. Hatteras--Fiction
7. Female Detective—Fiction  8. Detective—Fiction

If you enjoy this book and would like to discover how Angie Stallone began her career in the private investigation business, please check out my previous Outer Banks detective series (Weston Wolf Outer Banks Detective Series). In this three-book series, Angie teams up with Detective Weston Wolf to solve a variety of cases full of twists and turns. Also check out *A Nags Head Murder – An Angie Stallone Detective Novel.*

**Click on the links below to go to the Amazon Kindle page.**

# Weston Wolf Outer Banks Detective Series

These are stand-alone novels and can be read in any order.

**The Roanoke Island Murders: A Modern Retelling of the Maltese Falcon**

**The Singer in the Sound: A Weston Wolf OBX Detective Novel**

**Kitty Hawk Confidential: A Weston Wolf OBX Detective Novel**

Weston Wolf Outer Banks Detective – Three Book Set

You may be interested in my first Outer Banks series. If you enjoy the Outer Banks and reading murder mysteries, please check them out.

# Outer Banks Murder Series

These are stand-alone novels and can be read in any order.

The Healing Place (Prequel to Murder at Whalehead)

Book 1 – Murder at Whalehead

Book 2 – Murder at Hatteras

Book 3 – Murder on the Outer Banks

Book 4 – Murder at Ocracoke

Book 5 – The Treasure of Portstmouth Island

Outer Banks Murder Series 5-Book Set

A Nags Head Murder

# THE CORA TREE MURDER
## An Outer Banks Mystery

## Chapter 1

*I'm running slower than a turtle today.* Angie Stallone blinked sweat from her eyes as she focused on the edge of the road. *I've got two months before the race. Slow and steady, I'll be ready.* She turned onto Buccaneer Drive, ran a couple hundred yards and made a sharp left onto Snug Harbor Drive toward the Pamlico Sound. *Besides, no matter how slow I run, I'm still lapping everyone on the couch.* The mid-morning, late August sun cast her shadow in front of her. She glanced at her jangling form passing over the asphalt and chuckled to herself. *At least I can keep up with my shadow.*

Up ahead a patch of grass and a large live oak split the road. A woman stood in front of an ancient tree with her arms spread and hands pressed against its bark. She wore a crimson ankle-length dress, and her dark hair, streaked with gray, fluttered in the wind.

The woman stared into the tree's large hole. Above her, thick branches spread and extended over the road on both sides. A black cat weaved between her feet, rubbing its side against her shins.

*What is she doing? Must be Hug-a-Tree Thursday.* Beyond the tree, Angie noticed a group of teenagers heading in her direction. She slowed to a walk as the teens circled the tree.

A tall kid with a sparse mustache and long sandy hair called out, "Cora the Witch!"

*Oh no. Don't tell me they are going to pick on this old woman.* She stopped about thirty yards away.

The tall youth pointed at the cat. "Take your demon child and go back to hell."

Most of the teens laughed except for two girls who stood next to each other, a pretty blonde and a redhead with freckled cheeks. The tall blonde looked familiar. *Do I know her?* The woman straightened and backed away from the tree.

A dark-haired kid with bad acne said, "She stinks. They say witches cast spells, but she casts smells."

"You're a poor excuse for a poet, Zeke," the tall youth said. "But you're right. She smells like a dead dolphin. Get the hell out of here witch! We don't want you around."

"Yeah," the acne-faced kid said. He wore a black tank top imprinted with a white grinning skull and the word "Misfits" above it. "Get out of town, or we'll tie you to that tree and burn you down."

The red-haired girl frowned. "Leave her alone. She

knows about those kinds of things."

The tall kid sneered, "What kinds of things?"

"Witchcraft. I saw her collecting plants along the sound. She knows how to heal you or put a curse on you."

"You're full of crap." He turned away from the girl and took two steps toward the woman. "I told you to get out the hell out of here!"

As the woman backed away to where Angie stood, she mumbled indecipherable words.

"Listen!" a boy with a shaved head shouted. "She *is* putting a curse on us."

Angie stepped between the woman and the teens. "That's enough. She's not bothering you. Quit harassing her."

"Who the hell are you?" The tall youth jutted out his chest. "You can't tell us what to do."

"I'm a local detective, and my husband is a Dare County deputy."

"So what," he said. "The whole town knows this woman is a witch, and her cat is her demon child. We don't want her around here."

Angie furrowed her brow. "I don't care what people around here think. She has her rights, and you are breaking the law by hassling her. If you don't cease and desist, I will press charges against you and see you in court. What are your names?"

The teens backed away, and the tall one said, "Don't tell her your names. She's nobody. Let's go. She and the old witch can go to hell together." They turned and sauntered away.

Angie shook her head. *What a bunch of punks. Who was that blonde? I know I've seen her before.* She turned to face the woman. *She's gone. Where did she go?* She glanced down and saw the black cat staring up at her. *She left her cat behind. That's weird. It has six toes.*

Angie walked up to the tree and checked out the large cavity. *Why was she gazing into this hole?* The cat approached, meowed and clawed the trunk. Walking around the tree, she noticed letters carved into the bark. She reached and traced the letter "C" with her finger and then traced the others—O-R-A. *Cora. The kids called her Cora the Witch. It looks like the letters were burned into the bark.*

She felt the cat rub against her shins, knelt and rubbed the top of its head. *Tell me, Six-Toes, do you belong to Cora?* She noticed the cat wore a red collar with an unusual pendant—a round amber medallion with a silver letter A over an upside-down horseshoe. *Hmmmm. Obviously, you belong to somebody.*

# Chapter 2

Angie headed back to Route 12 at a slow pace. *Three miles to go. I'm beat. What a strange encounter. Teenagers can be so nasty. I feel bad for that old woman.* She trudged along for about a mile and noticed her shoe was untied. She slowed to a stop in a patch of grass in front Café Pamlico's parking lot. *I could use a tall glass of water.* She glanced at the restaurant, a yellow, two-story structure that looked more like a house than a fine eatery. *I'm sure they'd appreciate me dripping drops of sweat all over their entranceway.*

As she bent down to tie her shoe, something nudged her thigh. She heaved in a quick breath and stiffened. The black cat gazed up at her. "Why are you following me?" She shook her head. *Things are getting weirder.* She tied her shoe, stood and walked about twenty yards. The cat kept pace. *Okay, now what am I going to do? Keep running, I guess.* "Are you going to finish my workout with me?" She transitioned to a slow jog, and the cat tagged along.

For the next mile she thought about the woman and the tree. She remembered someone mentioning a legendary tree in Frisco but couldn't recall any details. *Was that the tree? Why was the name CORA burned into it? The old woman seemed to be entranced with whatever she saw in the hole. Maybe she was looking into another world.* Angie chuckled. *This seems like an episode of Stranger Things.*

Ahead on the left she saw Buxton Village Books, a quaint old one-story white house that Mee Mee Roberts turned into an independent bookstore decades ago. *Mee Mee will know something about that tree. She knows something about everything on this island.*

She mounted the few steps to the front stoop, and the cat clambered up with her. At the door she turned and said, "You can't come in the shop. Lay down on the porch and wait for me." To her surprise, the cat stretched out on the wooden deck in the sunshine and yawned. "Okay. Either you're highly intelligent or worn out from the run. I'm guessing you're just tired. If you're here when I leave, you can come home with me." The cat rested its head on its paws and closed its eyes.

Angie entered the store and saw Mee Mee arranging books on a nearby table. She wore a tan knee-length dress. A wiry brunette in her mid-sixties, she possessed the energy of a teenager. Her ponytail bobbed as she placed the books on the stacks. She turned and peered at Angie through her tortoiseshell framed glasses. "Who were you talking to out there?"

"A cat. It's been following me for the last three miles."

"It's probably a stray looking for a home."

"I don't think so. It has a collar."

Mee Mee walked to the door and eyed the cat. "You're right. It belongs to somebody."

"There was a woman leaning against an old tree in the middle of Snug Harbor Drive. I think the cat belongs to her."

Mee Mee turned and faced her. "The Cora Tree?"

"I guess. It had the letters C-O-R-A burned into its bark. Is that the legendary tree in Frisco?"

Mee Mee nodded. "That's the one. Was the woman middle-aged with gray streaks through her hair?"

"Yeah." Angie told her about defending the woman when the teens hassled her. "When I turned around, she was gone, and the cat was sitting there looking up at me."

"I know her. She has stopped in here a couple times and picked up books on herbs, shells, and natural remedies. She said her name was Cora."

"The same name that's on the tree."

Mee Mee bobbed her head. "She reminds me of a gypsy. It wouldn't surprise me if she owned a crystal ball."

"Do you know where she lives? I want to return the cat."

"Driving home last week, I saw her walking down Old Doctors Road."

"That road cuts through the Buxton Woods. I've

walked those trails. It's spooky in those woods."

Mee Mee grinned. "Spooky vibes fit right in with the woman and the legend of the tree."

Angie walked behind the counter and sat on a chair next to the register. "Tell me about the legend."

"Okay, I think I know the basics of the story." Mee Mee leaned against the counter. "In the early 1700s, a woman and her baby arrived in Frisco. She managed to build a rude cabin in the Buxton Woods away from the village. Rumors began to circulate about her and her child. Stories of the Salem Witch Trials had spread among the townspeople. It didn't take long for them to conclude that the woman practiced sorcery and witchcraft."

Angie raised her eyebrows. "Now isn't that an interesting coincidence. The teens accused her of being a witch."

"I'm sure they've heard the legend, and she fits the description."

"Go on with the story. What happened next."

"The rumors spread. Someone said she had touched a cow, and days later it quit producing milk. A boy teased her at the village market. Not long after that he became ill and almost died. She was known to catch an abundance of fish, but the Frisco fishermen weren't having the same luck.

"Then a battered ship named the *Susan G.* arrived. It had a crew of ruffians and ex-slaves from Barbados. The captain, Eli Blood, was a Salem Massachusetts native. He hung out in the middle of town and hob-knobbed with the gossipers and busybodies. He bragged about being a witch hunter and protector of the people.

"After hearing the stories about Cora, he became suspicious. Then the body of a local fisherman washed up on shore. His face was frozen in terror and the numbers 666 were carved into his forehead. Captain Blood noticed that footprints surrounded the body. He followed them into the woods near where Cora had built her cabin. Then he resolved to lead the people of Frisco on a witch hunt to save them from her evil intentions.

Angie raked her fingers through her pixie-cut beige-blonde hair. "This story doesn't sound like it has a happy ending."

"Not really." Mee Mee took a deep breath. "Blood led an angry mob through the woods to Cora's cabin. They broke down the door, seized Cora and snatched up her baby. He led them to the middle of town and stopped by a large live oak. There he performed his first test. He took out his knife, lifted a lock of her hair and tried to cut it. Her hair was stronger than wire. Next, they tied her hands and feet and threw her into the Pamlico Sound, but she floated to the top.

"He recruited a few men from the village for the final test. The captain took out his witch hunting bowl and filled it with water. Then he pricked his finger and let a drop of blood fall into the bowl. His three recruits did the same. After stirring the water, he gazed into the bowl and said, 'There, see for yourself. It's the witch's face in the bosom of Satan.' The three men peered into the bowl and confirmed the vision.

"The townspeople gasped and called for her execution. Captain Blood tied Cora and her child to the tree. As his crew collected kindling and branches, dark clouds gathered over the town.

"A local resident, Captain Thomas Smith, protested. He said that Cora should be taken to the mainland and tried in a proper court of law. As Captain Blood reached to touch flame to the stack of wood, Smith grabbed his arm. Thunder rumbled, and Captain Blood shook his arm free.

"A bolt of lightning struck the tree, and thunder erupted again like the roar of a monster. Everyone was thrown to the ground, and dark smoke bellowed from the tree. The smoke slowly cleared, but to the villagers' surprise, Cora and the child had vanished. The ropes still hung on the trunk. The lightning bolt had ripped open a heart-shaped hole in the middle of the tree. The letters C-O-R-A were burned into the spot where Cora had been tied with her baby. A black cat appeared near the trunk of the tree, and the witnesses claimed her demon child transfigured into the cat."

Angie stood, walked to the door and stared at the cat asleep on the stoop. "Her demon child, you say?"

"That's the story."

Angie faced Mee Mee. "Do you want to go with me tomorrow when I return the child to Cora? I mean the cat."

"Sure. I'm always up for a walk through spooky woods."

"I have a feeling present-day Cora and the Cora of legend are somehow connected."

Mee Mee chuckled. "Let's see. There's Captain Blood, Captain Smith and you, the third captain."

"The third captain?"

"Captain Obvious."

# Chapter 3

Angie stepped out of the bookstore, and the black cat arose, stretched and rubbed its side against her leg. "You're still waiting for me, huh? Good. I want to find out if Cora is your owner. Do you think you can last another six hundred yards? I'll take it easy on you and walk the rest of the way home."

The cat stared up at her as if it understood every word.

"Let's go." Angie headed down Route 12 and veered left onto Rocky Rollinson Road. As if on a mission, the cat kept up. Most of the houses along the narrow lane sat propped on posts over grassy lots. About half of them were pre-fab, hauled in by trucks and placed onto their wooden supports high enough to keep frequent flood waters from reaching the living quarters. Angie loved her neighborhood and the good-hearted, working-class families that populated it.

She and her husband Joel had purchased their

home, a three-bedroom ranch, six years ago. Their daughter Phoebe came along a year later. Their lot was graced by the shade of several myrtles and sprawling live oaks. Joel's job as a deputy sheriff and the business generated by her detective agency provided income to pay the bills and make minor home improvements. Angie didn't mind the struggle. She loved her husband, her work, and the light of her life — her blue-eyed blonde daughter. Living on the edge of the ocean in a small tourist town was invigorating, challenging and fulfilling.

When Phoebe saw her mom walking up the driveway, she leapt out of the turtle-shaped sandbox and charged toward her. She skidded to a stop when she saw the black cat. "Mom! A kitty! Is she for me?"

"Sorry, Phoebe. It belongs to someone else, and I think it's a he."

Phoebe knelt next to the cat and stroked its head and back. The cat purred. "He likes me."

"You can help take care of him today, but tomorrow morning I have to find his owner. Come on. It's almost lunchtime. Let's get something to eat." They headed for the front door, climbed the few steps and entered the house. The cat walked in like he owned the place.

When they entered the kitchen, her husband said, "Hey, babe, how was the run?" About six feet tall with short sandy hair, Joel Thomas stood next to the open dishwasher, repositioning cups on the top rack. His white tank top and gray shorts fit snugly on his chiseled body.

"Slow but eventful."

"Race day in Raleigh will be here before you know it."

"I've got another two months to get ready."

"Look, Daddy," Phoebe said. "A cat followed Mommy home."

Joel turned from the dishwasher and appraised the cat.

"I call him Six Toes," Angie said. "I think he belongs to a woman named Cora." She recounted the confrontation with the teenagers and the sudden disappearance of the strange woman.

"I've had some run-ins with those kids, too. They're trouble." Joel scratched the three-day growth on his jaw. "I think I've seen that cat before at the Frisco Sandwich Company. He bums food from the patrons who sit at the picnic tables. He's one of the island's polydactyls."

"Polywhat?"

"Polydactyls. Six-toed cats. There's a bunch on the island."

"Why?"

"It's a cool story. Have you ever heard of a ghost ship called the Carroll A. Deering?"

"Of course. That's the one that wrecked just off Cape Point back in the 1920s."

"Right. Several rescue attempts were made by the men from the life-saving station. When they finally reached the stranded vessel, they discovered the captain and crew were missing. To this day, nobody knows what happened to them. In the galley they found food prepared for the crew's next meal. One surfmen discovered a six-toed cat on board. He took the cat ashore, and it eventually produced a generation of six-toed cats on Hatteras Island."

Phoebe rubbed the black cat's cheeks. "So, Mr. Six Toes came from a ghost ship?"

Joel laughed. "His great-great-great-great grandfather did."

"I don't think he's a stray," Angie said. "Look at his collar."

Phoebe tugged on the amber pendant. "It's so pretty."

She stood above her daughter and stared at the medallion. "If it doesn't belong to Cora, then it must belong to some family in the Snug Harbor neighborhood."

"Do you know where she lives?" Joel asks.

"I have an idea. I'll pick up Mee Mee tomorrow morning, and we'll head down Old Doctors Road. Mee Mee thinks she lives somewhere in the Buxton Woods."

"Watch for snakes," Joel said. "There're rattlers and moccasins in those woods."

"I'll watch where I step. How about you? You said your new assignment might be risky. Have they given you any details yet?"

Joel nodded. "It's going to be a great opportunity for me, but there is an element of danger."

Angie took a slow breath and narrowed her eyes. "I don't like the sound of that. What do they want you to do?"

"They're offering me a detective position. With all the cocaine traffic and fentanyl overdoses on the island, the DEA believes a Mexican cartel has set up shop in a house in Hatteras or Frisco. My main focus will be gathering evidence on locations, identifying the main trafficker and his dealers on this end of the Outer Banks. I'll be collaborating with a federal agent."

Angie turned towards her daughter. "Phoebe, please go to your room and pick up your toys. After you clean your room and I take my shower, we'll eat lunch."

"Can I take Mr. Six Toes with me?"

"No. You can play with Mr. Six Toes after your room is cleaned up."

"Aw, Mom."

Angie pointed to the hallway. "Go!"

"Don't complain, Ladybug," Joel said. "I'll cook up something delicious. What would like?"

"Easy-peasy-mac-n-cheesy."

"You got it."

Phoebe stood, skipped out of the kitchen and down the hallway.

"I didn't want her to hear any more of this conversation," Angie said. "Those Mexican cartels are deadly."

"I know, especially if they're competing with

other gangs for real estate. They'll kill rivals and anyone else who gets in their way. No remorse."

"They are also known for human trafficking."

Joel nodded. "True. If they establish a stronghold here, everyone will suffer. More drugs, more deaths, more heartache."

Angie thought about the kids who circled the tree. "And some of the local teenagers will get swept up into it."

"I bet they already are involved. Kids do drugs. They have connections. They sell dope. Teens would be high on the list of recruits."

"Well . . . you always wanted to be a detective. I'm happy for you, but remember, you've got a wife and young daughter."

Joel reached and drew her into his arms. "I'll be careful." He clasped the back of her head and kissed her, a firm wet kiss. "Maybe we can start working on the next one, a son this time."

"Maybe." Angie winked at him. "If you get a good pay raise."

"I'll demand it." He slid his hand down her back. "You're sweaty. You need a shower."

"That's where I'm heading now."

When Angie entered her daughter's bedroom, she frowned. Phoebe sat on the floor facing six stuffed animals — two teddy bears, an owl, a fox, a raccoon and a unicorn. "I thought I told you to put your toys away."

Phoebe glanced up at her. "I will, Mommy, but

first we have to learn our ABCs."

"You already know your ABCs. You need to learn to pick up your toys."

"But school starts on Monday, and I'm practicing with my friends."

"Come on." Angie reached down and picked up the unicorn. "I'll help you. Let's get this room in order, and then you can go out and check on Mr. Six Toes."

"That's a good plan."

After helping Phoebe straighten up her bedroom, Angie headed to the shower. The warm water felt good on her sweat-cooled body. As the spray pelted her back, she imagined Joel wearing a black polo shirt with the Dare County Sheriff's Department logo—the Cape Hatteras Lighthouse against a blue Atlantic. *He'd look good in that shirt. He looks good in any shirt.* She wanted another child. *I'm thirty. Time is ticking away.* She closed her eyes and smiled. *Yeah, it's time to start working on baby number two.* As she shampooed and rinsed her hair, she tried to relax all the muscles in her body. *I can't stress out over what may or may not happen in life. We both chose the path we're on. Whatever comes, we'll handle it.*

After showering and drying her hair, she slipped into a sage green sleeveless romper and headed to the kitchen. Phoebe sat at the Formica-topped table gobbling her macaroni and cheese. The cat, standing near Phoebe's chair, feasted on turkey leftovers.

Joel delivered a large plate of cheesy pasta to her

end of the table. "Carbos for my half marathoner."

"Thanks. Toss in a banana, and I'll be happier than a monkey on a vine."

"Coming right up." Joel pivoted, swiped a banana off the counter next to the sink, and handed it to her. A rapping sound reverberated from the front entryway. "Someone's at the door. You two enjoy my gourmet meal. I'll see who's here."

"Okay, Gordon Ramsay. You're more cheesy than this macaroni."

Joel laughed as he hurried to the entry hall.

Phoebe scooped up her last bite, downed it and slid off the chair.

"How about a banana or an apple?" Angie coaxed.

"No thanks. I want to play with Six Toes."

The cat mewed and glanced up at the girl.

Footsteps sounded down the hallway, and Joel walked into the kitchen. Following him, a tall blonde teenager with a familiar face entered and stood next to him.

"We have a guest," Joel said. "A neighbor from down the road, Miss Sammy Cline. She says she needs to talk to you."

Hearing the name, Angie knew immediately who she was.

# Chapter 4

"Now I remember you," Angie said.

The pretty blonde with a petite nose and dark brown eyes hung her head. She wore white shorts that exposed her long legs and a Billie Eilish t-shirt. "I'm sorry about the way my friends acted at the Cora Tree."

"No need to apologize. You didn't harass the woman like the others. Besides that, you saved my life once."

She met Angie's gaze and nodded. "The first time I saw you in the neighborhood, I remembered. My mom and I lived in a house along Historic Cottage Row in Nags Head."

Angie stood. "I was being pursued by a homicidal maniac through that neighborhood. I pounded on your door, and you let me in. Then you hid me in your attic."

Joel's eyes widened as he turned toward the teenager. "You're that Sammy?"

She nodded. "I was eleven years old back then."

Angie stepped toward her and hugged her. "You've become a beautiful young woman." They separated, and Angie patted her cheek and smiled.

"Thank you. My mom ran into financial problems, and we had to sell the house in Nags Head. We moved here three months ago, about a quarter mile down the road."

"So, you've been making friends with the local teens since you moved here?" Angie asked.

"Yes. I met a girl named Kiara Bailey on the beach back in June, and she introduced me to the rest of the gang. I was the new kid on the block, and they invited me to hang out."

Joel cleared his throat. "Why did they pick on the woman at the tree?"

"John doesn't like her."

Joel furrowed his brow. "John who?"

"John Stokes."

"I'm guessing he's the leader," Angie said, "the tall kid with the wispy mustache."

She bobbed her head. "His dad told him the story about Cora the Witch. We've seen her at the tree several times. He says she's the real deal and has come here to curse the town."

"Do you believe that?" Joel asked.

"No, and I don't think he does either. He just doesn't want her around." She took a step forward and crouched next to Phoebe and the cat. "Is this her cat? I recognize the red collar."

Phoebe patted the cat's head and smiled. "This is Six Toes. He followed Mommy home. My name is Phoebe."

"It's nice to meet you Phoebe." She rubbed the cat's cheek. "I'm Sammy."

"Was the cat with the woman whenever you saw her at the tree?" Angie asked.

Sammy glanced up at her. "Yes. John said the cat was her demon child. I guess that's part of the legend."

Angie tilted her head. "Then the cat *must* belong to her. You don't know where she lives, do you?"

"One of the guys said she lives along the Pinecone Path in the Buxton Woods, and that worries me."

"Why?" Joel asked.

She stood. "Those boys like to play pranks on people, mean pranks. Since John said he doesn't want her around, they've been planning something. I'm not sure what, but I know they're out to punk her. That's another reason I came here today. I thought maybe you could warn her."

"I hope to visit her tomorrow and return her cat. You must not be as enthralled with John Stokes as the rest of them."

She shrugged. "He gave me a ride home today. I think he likes me."

"Do you like him?" Angie asked.

"He's cute, but I don't know how I feel about him."

Angie raised an eyebrow. "I'd be careful around him if I were you."

"On the way home, he stopped at the Cora Tree."

"Why?" Angie asked.

"He got out of the car and looked in the tree's hole. Then he came back with a note. I asked him what was on the note, and he said it was just a message someone left him. I got a glimpse of it before he stuck it in his pocket."

"What was on it?" Joel asked.

"A picture of a tall tower with some words underneath and a number-1245. I couldn't make out the words."

Angie shifted her focus to Joel. "That's interesting."

Joel scratched his chin. "Uh huh."

"Then something else happened. Halfway home he turned off on a side road that led into some woods. He took out a joint, lit it up and offered it to me."

"Did you take a drag?" Joel asked.

She shook her head. "I don't smoke dope. Every once in a while I'll drink a beer at their parties, but I don't do drugs."

Angie said, "Do they?"

She directed her eyes to the floor. "Some of them do. Mostly pills, something they call Adam and Eve."

Joel raised a finger. "That's Ecstasy."

"Do they do cocaine?" Angie asked.

She looked up at her. "Sometimes."

Angie touched her shoulder. "You need to break away from those kids."

"I'm going to try, but once you're in, it's hard to get out. I don't want to get John mad at me."

Angie tensed her eyebrows. "What would he do?"

Sammy took a halting breath. "He's unpredictable. I've seen him slap his girlfriend. When he finished the joint in the car, he put his arm around me and wanted to make out. I pulled away. I thought he was going to hit me. I told him I couldn't do that to my friend Kiara. She's in love with him. I know they have . . . you know . . . done the . . ." She glanced at Phoebe.

Angie said, "I get it. What did he say?"

"He said they broke up that morning, but I didn't believe him. I told him I'd think about going on a date with him, but I wanted to talk to Kiara first. He seemed ticked off but didn't hurt me. Then he changed his tune and became all friendly again. It was weird. After he dropped me off, I decided to come down here and talk to you."

"I'm glad you did," Angie said. "We're here for you. Be careful around Stokes. Let us know if you need our help."

"I will."

"Listen," Joel said. "If you overhear any plans to hurt Cora, please let us know. She doesn't deserve any kind of abuse from those boys."

Sammy closed her eyes and grimaced. "I know. She's just a harmless old lady. I'll keep my eyes and ears open when I'm hanging out with them. Maybe I can break away from the gang slowly without making waves."

"Good idea," Angie said. "Watch your step and be smart."

"Thanks for listening to me." She reached down

and caressed Phoebe's cheek. "Nice meeting you, Phoebe."

"You, too," Phoebe said. "And you're really pretty."

"Thanks." She turned to Angie, hugged her, said goodbye and walked into the family room and out the front door.

Joel circled the table and sat down on one of the yellow-padded chairs. "Do you want to know what I think?"

Angie sat across from him. "Enlighten me."

"John Stokes is a dealer, and that tree is a contact point."

Angie bobbed her head. "You might be right. We shouldn't jump to conclusions, but it makes sense. He doesn't want Cora hanging out at the tree. She might be in the way when he comes to pick up a message from his distributor. If it's not well hidden, she may even find it."

Phoebe stood and tugged on Angie's elbow. "If Mr. Six Toes doesn't belong to that lady, can we keep him?"

Angie gently pinched her chin. "Mr. Six Toes can stay with us until I find his owner."

"Really?"

"Really. But don't get your hopes up. I think he belongs to Cora. Tomorrow morning I'm going to find out where she lives and have a good talk with her."

"Mommy." Phoebe's eyes grew wide. "Do you think Cora is a good witch or a bad witch?"

Angie chuckled. "I hope she's a good witch."

# Chapter 5

A brisk morning breeze sent a shiver through Angie as she led the cat down the driveway. She loved her Jeep Gladiator. She purchased the car a year ago, a 2020 model with 60,000 miles. It was a big step up from the ancient Honda Civic she had traded in. She wanted a car she could drive onto the beach for the fun of it. Phoebe loved picnics along the seashore, and Joel fished occasionally. Rumbling over the sand gave her that wonderful feeling of freedom from the road. The Gladiator easily managed the shifting sands of the Hatteras Island shoreline.

When Angie opened the passenger door, Six Toes sprung onto the seat and curled up as if part of the daily routine. Angie shook her head. *That is an unusual cat.* As she drove down Rocky Rollinson Road, the sun's light streamed through the overhanging trees creating a patchwork of light and shadow. Butterflies and dragonflies caught the piercing rays on their flittering wings. Most of the houses sat back from the narrow road with pickup trucks and well-worn cars parked in their driveways. An occasional pond or canal broke up the thick greenery to the left or right.

Pulling onto Route 12, she smiled. Joel had cooked a pancake breakfast, and Phoebe had devoured four of them. *I bet that girl grows four inches this year. Kindergarten starts on Monday. That'll be a big transition.* With Joel's schedule, Angie got her work done in the morning and kept her eye on Phoebe in the afternoon. He'd get home from his shift about nine, and they'd watch some TV and the news together before calling it a day. Life had settled into a comfortable schedule.

With tourist season still in high gear, the traffic in the bustling village was steady but not sluggish. In a few weeks things would settle down. The drive to Mee Mee's bookstore only took a couple minutes. Small signs on the edge of the road named Buxton's historic houses: Dillon House, White Oaks, Miller House, Kit-Mamie House and Maude Estus House. The white-painted craftsman, saltbox and Cape Cod style homes gave the village a welcoming charm and contrasted with the modern three-story vacation rentals that dominated the oceanfront.

At half past ten, the parking spaces in front of the bookstore were occupied by customers. Angie parked in front of the guest house, a property Mee Mee bought several years ago. The purchase offered more parking, room to store inventory and a place for friends and traveling writers to stay when visiting. Angie beeped her horn, and the cat sat up.

Mee Mee exited the store, scampered down the few steps, turned right and hurried to the Jeep. She opened the passenger door and noticed the cat. "Hey, Fuzzball, you're in my seat."

The cat responded with a quizzical look.

Mee Mee laughed. "If cats could talk, they wouldn't." She picked up the cat, climbed onto the seat, rested the cat on her lap and managed to buckle her seat belt. "Let's get going."

Angie backed onto the road. "Who's minding the store?"

"Kathy. Lots of customers this morning, but she can handle it. How's the private eye business?"

"Slow. I've got to do some background checks on potential hires for an investment firm. I can catch up on that this afternoon at home. Believe it or not, most of the work I do is boring."

"Maybe this visit to the Cora Tree lady will add some excitement to your day."

The cat meowed.

Angie glimpsed the cat, smiled and said, "Six Toes thinks so. Yesterday afternoon was interesting." Angie recounted the details of Sammy's visit and the girl's worry that some of the teenage boys may prank the strange woman.

Mee Mee shook her head. "Sounds like history is about to repeat itself. People who don't fit in get persecuted. The Cora of legend sure did. Of course, legends aren't always historically accurate."

"I'm curious to find out the connection between her

and the Cora of legend."

Mee Mee couldn't help snickering. "Maybe Cora came back through a time portal, you know, one of those worm holes."

"Right, and an apple a day will keep the doctor away if you throw it hard enough."

"Funny you mention the word doctor." She pointed to her left. "Old Doctors Road is coming up. Maybe you ought to be a psychic."

"Nope. I don't see any future in it."

Angie made a left onto the unpaved, one-lane track. She drove about a hundred yards through overhanging live oaks and pines before finding a spot wide enough to pull off to the side. An abundance of dwarf palmettos sprang up amidst the surrounding thickets, giving the maritime forest a deep southern feel. The screeches and calls of a variety of birds pierced through the thick air.

Angie opened her door and stepped onto the sandy lane. The cat clambered over the storage console, onto the driver's seat and followed her out the door. "How'd this road get its name? Did a doctor live in these woods at one time?"

"Yep," Mee Mee said, wading through ferns as she circled the car. "Old Doc Garlic lived in a cabin down one of these paths decades ago."

A thick cloud doused the sun's rays, casting a sudden gloom on the surroundings. Angie panned the darkening foliage. "Doc Garlic? Don't people use garlic to ward off vampires?"

"Don't worry about vampires in these woods. Too much competition."

"Huh?"

Mee Mee laughed. "Mosquitos."

Angie swatted a bug in front of her face. "Let's get moving before those bloodsuckers get to us."

They walked briskly along the sandy road for several hundred yards, peering through the woods to catch a glimpse of Cora's hut.

"There's over a thousand acres in these woods," Mee Mee said. "How are we going to find her place?"

"Have you ever heard of the Pinecone Path?"

"Sure. There's a lot of loblolly pines along that trail."

"Sammy told us she overheard a couple boys saying Cora lived along that path. They must have followed her to find out where she lived."

Mee Mee pointed ahead. "It's not far from here. Maybe another sixty or seventy yards."

When they reached the path, Angie peered up at several towering loblolly pines. Glancing down, she noticed a multitude of huge pinecones scattered across the path's opening.

"This is the one," Mee Mee said. "It goes back into the woods for quite a stretch."

Six Toes cut in between them and traipsed along the trail. Angie waved toward the cat. "Follow the leader."

The scrub thickets and sedges grew thicker and the environs darker as they progressed deeper into the woods. Ancient live oaks extended their branches above them like sentinels incensed at their intrusion. Angie glanced over her shoulder. "You said you were up for a walk through a spooky forest."

"Shhhhhh. Did you hear that?"

Angie tilted her head. "Sounds like a violin."

Mee Mee pointed to a trail up ahead that branched off to the right. "It's coming from that direction."

The cat turned onto the trail.

"Must be the way to go," Angie said. After making their way along the twisting path for a couple minutes, she stopped abruptly. "There! I see a small cabin through the trees." The strains of the violin moaned the long notes of some mournful sonata.

"I wonder if that's Old Doc Garlic's place. She might have fixed it up."

"Maybe. Let's check it out." Approaching the rustic shelter, Angie spied the form of a person through a side window slowly sliding a bow across the instrument's strings. The whine of the note sent a jittering chill down her spine.

Constructed of thick logs with a moss-covered roof, the cabin could have been excerpted from the pages of a Grimm's fairy tale. A stovepipe rose up from the back, and steel gray smoke poured out and gathered above the cabin amidst the tree branches. They stepped up on the front stoop. Mee Mee made a fist and pounded on the windowless door. The music stopped.

After a few seconds the door opened slightly, and

Cora glared at them, dark eyes narrowing. With a gruff voice she said, "What do you want?"

# Chapter 6

The cat mewed. Cora glanced down and smiled. "There you are, Midnight. Where have you been? You always come back to me."

"He followed me home yesterday after you disappeared," Angie said.

She squinted at Angie. "You were at the tree. I'm sorry. I wanted to get out of there. Those kids are a thorn in my soul." She opened the door halfway, and the cat sauntered in. Her pale face contrasted with the dark bags under her eyes, thick black eyebrows and red lips. The gray streaks in her wiry hair matched the pallor of her complexion. A loose-fitting crimson dress hung limply on her medium build and reached to her ankles. "I want to thank you for defending me. Most people around here despise me."

"Do you remember me?" Mee Mee asked.

She shifted her focus to Mee Mee. "Of course. You're from the bookstore." She opened the door wider and stepped back. "Please come in."

Angie glanced around the dim interior as she walked into the one-room hovel. Windows centered on each side let in meager shafts of light. Shelves lined the walls displaying shells, bottles filled with strange liquids, and jars containing herbs and plants. A wooden chair sat beside the left window with a violin and bow propped against its backrest. A round weathered table with three more wooden chairs stood in the middle of the room.

Cora swept her hand toward the table. "Please, sit down."

Mee Mee pulled out a chair. "We haven't introduced ourselves. I'm Mee Mee Roberts, and this is Angie Stallone Thomas."

The woman bobbed her head slowly. "Nice to make your acquaintance. My name is Cora Mangas."

Angie sat down. "You have the same first name as the woman from the Cora Tree legend."

"I am a descendant."

"Really?" Mee Mee said. "How do you know?"

She leaned on the table. "From stories my great grandmother told me and research of family history. My mother named me after her, and I've always felt a strong link to her."

"Is that why you moved here?" Angie asked.

She nodded. "I was drawn here. I needed to make a connection to the past. The first time I touched the tree I felt her presence."

Angie panned the room. "You've gathered an interesting collection of items on your shelves. Are these local shells and plants?"

"Most of them. You'd be surprised at what the earth offers us. I honor the life-giving and healing properties of nature. Like my ancestor, I am committed to living in balance with the earth. Would you like to try some of my Bee Palm Tea? I brew it from the monarda plant. I have some ready on the stove."

The muscles around Angie's mouth tightened, but Mee Mee shrugged and said, "Sure. We'll give it a go."

Angie flashed her an uneasy glance.

Cora opened a cabinet stationed near the right window and removed a tray and three cups. Carrying the tray and cups, she waddled to a woodstove at the back of the room, lifted a kettle and poured the steaming liquid into the cups. She plodded back to the table, lowered the tray, distributed the cups and sat down.

Angie tried a sip. *Not bad.* It had a mild, minty taste. She took a bigger drink. *Wow. It actually tastes pretty good.*

"Do you like it?" Cora asked.

"Yes." Angie said. "It's delicious."

"Excellent," Mee Mee agreed.

After several minutes of sipping tea and conversations about local plants and their healing properties, the room quieted. Angie placed her cup on the table. "When I saw you yesterday, you were leaning on the tree and staring into the hole."

"That is where the lightning struck. When I look

deeply into that hole, I can see things."

Mee Mee scooted her chair forward. "What kind of things?"

"Things from the past and things in the future. I saw what happened at the tree hundreds of years ago, and I can see what will happen."

Angie raised an eyebrow. *This is starting to get weirder.* "So, you can . . . envision the future by looking into that hole?"

She nodded. "I have the gift of divination. The tree is one point of contact, but I can also see into a person's soul and discern many things. Would you like me to demonstrate?"

Angie straightened. "Sure."

"Have you finished your tea?"

"Just about."

Cora pulled a tattered handkerchief from her dress pocket and placed it in front of Angie. "Swirl your cup three times and place it upside down on the cloth."

"Okay." Looking into the cup, she noticed tea leaves in the bottom.

"Swirl it three times," Cora ordered.

Angie swirled the cup, counting each rotation, and turned it over onto the handkerchief.

Cora extended her hands as if to receive a precious offering. "Your aura has directed the formation of the tea leaves at the bottom of the cup." She reached and drew the cup and cloth toward her. Then she rotated the cup three times, turned it over and examined the formation of the leaves. She took slow breaths and closed her eyes.

"What do you see?" Angie asked.

Cora raised her chin and met her gaze. "You are married, and you have a daughter."

Angie swallowed and nodded. "Go on."

"You are deeply in love with your husband, but you are worried about him. He faces danger daily."

A cold wave flowed over Angie, but then she remembered telling the teenagers that her husband was a deputy sheriff. *She must have heard me, but how does she know about our daughter?*

"The danger . . ." Her eyes narrowed. ". . . the danger he faces may increase in the near future."

*Joel's new assignment. Is she just guessing?* "My husband is a law enforcement officer. He risks his life every day."

"Forces of evil have gathered on this island. They have no regard for the law. He must be careful."

"What kind of forces?" Mee Mee asked.

"Dark forces from the depths of hell." She clasped her hands across the top of her head. "I see someone else . . . a girl . . . very pretty."

Sammy's face flashed in Angie's mind. "What about her?"

"She came to your house recently. She had something important to tell you."

"Do you recognize her?"

Cora closed her eyes and tilted her head back. "Yes. She was at the tree with the teenagers."

"Her name is Sammy. She came to my house to

apologize for her friends' behavior."

Cora lowered her head and opened her eyes. "But that's not all she had to say."

Angie nodded. "She wanted me to warn you about something she overheard."

Cora folded her hands on the tabletop. "Her friends are plotting against me."

Angie nodded. "Sammy overheard some of the boys talking about playing a prank on you. She didn't know the details, but she fears they may go too far."

"They are out to get me."

"Why?" Mee Mee said. "Why do these kids harass you?"

"Because they fear what they don't understand."

"What about their leader, the tall boy?" Angie said. "He seems especially annoyed with you."

"Yes. He doesn't want me near the tree. He knows I have powers. He knows I can see into his soul."

"My husband is familiar with those kids. They've caused some trouble in town. I'll tell him to alert the other deputies about what they're up to."

Cora wobbled her head. "I don't fear those boys." She motioned toward the shelves. "My knowledge and powers exceed the intended harm of their childish schemes.  Those who seek to do me wrong will regret their decision."

Midnight leapt onto the table, and Angie flinched, her body tensing from head to toe. Cora pulled the cat onto her lap and stroked its head. "There, now, Midnight," she said. "Don't fret. Long ago when they tried to harm Cora, lightning struck."

# Chapter 7

On the first day of kindergarten Angie did her best to keep from crying. She didn't want Phoebe to see the tears and held them off until Mrs. Riley and the children were settled in the classroom and the door closed. Then she hurried to her car, avoiding the other parents, climbed onto the seat, shut the door and bawled. *My little girl is growing up. How does the old song go? Turn around, and you're three. Turn around, and you're four. Turn around, and you're a young one going out of the door.*

Cape Hatteras Elementary School was located on Middle Ridge Road, less than a mile from Mee Mee's bookstore. She decided to stop by the shop and say hello before heading home to spend the morning staring at a computer screen to research a court case and complete a couple background checks. She pulled into a parking space in front of the store and checked her face in the visor mirror. *No tear streaks. Good.* She got out of the Jeep and headed to the entrance. The breeze wavered the American flag that hung from the store's sign and ruffled the red geraniums that grew from large ceramic pots near the steps and sprung from hanging baskets slung from the porch posts.

Entering the store, she saw Mee Mee behind the register checking out a customer, a tall man wearing a camouflage bucket hat. As he headed out the door, she said, "How's the kindergarten mom doing? Did you hit the detachment wall?"

"Yeah, like a marathoner with six miles to go."

Mee Mee smiled. "How'd my Ladybug hold up?"

"She's a rock. Gave me a hug and walked into the classroom without looking back."

"Sometimes kids adapt to new circumstances better than we do."

"True."

"What's up?"

"Just came by to say hi. It's been almost a week since we visited Cora. Has she stopped in here?"

"No, but I've been thinking about her. That was a most unusual encounter. Do you think she's a charlatan or a soothsayer?"

Angie drifted behind the counter and sat on a stool. "Somehow, she took the information she gathered at the tree and came up with an accurate picture of my homelife."

"A good con can do that."

"But how did she know about my daughter and Sammy's visit?"

"I have no idea. Maybe she is a psychic. There have

been documented cases where psychics helped the FBI solve crimes."

Angie shrugged. "Maybe psychics are good guessers. She did seem concerned about crime on the island."

"Right. She mentioned dark forces from hell. What do you think she meant by that?"

"I haven't run into any demons lately, but there has been a slew of fentanyl overdoses up and down the Outer Banks. People are dropping like flies. Joel has been assigned to a drug task force."

"So, the dark forces from hell are drug dealers?"

"Dealers and suppliers. Sammy told us most of her friends do drugs. I'm wondering if Cora somehow picked up on that while staring into the hole at the tree."

"What do you mean? Do you think she had some kind of vision of pills or pot or maybe the Grim Reaper holding a hypodermic needle?"

"No. Sammy told us that John Stokes retrieved a message from the hole. He's the leader of the pack. Since Cora hangs out at the tree, she may have noticed suspicious activity."

Mee Mee raised a finger. "Or even found a note?"

"It's possible. Maybe she wants to be one of those psychics who help solve crimes."

"Could be. Knowing you and Joel are in the business, she has made a connection with the right people. But is she a psychic or pseudo-psychic?"

"Good question. If I had a Magic 8-Ball, I'd give you

an answer."

Mee Mee chuckled. "I've got a Magic 8-Ball app on my phone." She dipped her hand into the back pocket of her jeans, slid out her phone and activated the app. "There."

"What does it say?"

She raised her eyebrows. "Ask again later."

"Figures. Your 8-Ball app ain't worth crap." Angie stood. "I'm heading home. I've got some work to catch up on before I pick up Phoebe later this afternoon."

"Give a hug to Ladybug for me. Tell her I have a new book for her next time she comes to the store."

"Will do." Angie waved and headed out the door.

***

When Angie entered the kitchen, she caught sight of Joel finishing up the morning dishes. His tight black slacks and deputy shirt gave him that hard-edged look she found quite appealing. He closed the dishwasher, turned and said, "Well, how'd it go?"

"'Bout as well as expected."

"Did Phoebe put up a fuss?"

"Are you kidding? She walked into that classroom like she owned the place."

Joel smiled, dimples forming at the corners of his mouth. "Like mother, like daughter."

"Not quite. I cried like a kid who just watched her ice cream fall off the cone."

Joel stepped closer. "Do you need a hug?"

"I could always use a hug."

They embraced, and he pulled her close. She felt his heart beating against her cheek and whiffed the musky scent of his aftershave. When she gazed up, he kissed her, a long tender kiss. A warm sensation almost melted her. When their lips broke apart, she said, "You smell good."

He grinned. "I do my best."

"Nobody does it better."

She stepped back, breaking the embrace. "What's the latest news from work? Did you meet with the DEA guy yet?"

"I have an appointment with him this afternoon. His name is Tim Shepherd."

"I like the name. Hopefully, he'll share some information to help with your assignment."

"He might. Unfortunately, there are no short cuts. Investigations like this take time. We'll try to identify and arrest the local dealers and hope to get feedback from them. However, they usually don't squeal on their suppliers, especially if a Mexican cartel is involved. That would be a death wish."

"At least you have one lead on a possible dealer — the Stokes boy."

Joel furrowed his brow, eyes tensing. "Yeah. What's his first name?"

"John."

Joel extracted his cellphone from his pants pocket, tapped it a couple times and then scrolled. "Here it is. I got a message from Sheriff Thompson this morning about a missing girl. Hearing that name rang a bell."

"How so?"

"Didn't Sammy tell us that Stokes had a girlfriend?"

Angie nodded. "She said Stokes claimed he broke up with her."

"Do you remember her name?"

Angie closed her eyes. "Kiara something . . . Kiara Bailey?"

"That's it." Joel pointed at his phone. "That's the name of the missing girl."

# Chapter 8

After dinner, Angie made sure Phoebe completed her worksheets – an ABC practice page and a connect-the-dots picture of the Cape Hatteras Lighthouse. *Golly, I don't remember ever having kindergarten homework when I was a kid. Times have changed.* She thought about the fentanyl scourge devastating families along the Outer Banks and shook her head. *It's definitely not the world I grew up in. Kids have become prey for predators and pushers.* Kiara Bailey's face, her freckled cheeks and flowing red hair, flared in her mind. *I can't imagine what her family is going through right now. No doubt about it. Times have changed.*

Phoebe drew the final line from dot 24 to dot 25 at the top of the lighthouse. "There! All done with my homework. Can I watch some YouTube videos on my iPad?"

"No way. You're getting addicted to that iPad."

"Aw, Mommy. I want to watch Blimpo. He's funny."

"You help me fold all the towels, and I'll think about it."

Phoebe frowned. "Can we watch TV while we fold?"

"Yeah. We'll watch the evening news."

"Booooooo. I want to watch Bluesie."

"Come on. Let's go get those towels."

Angie retrieved the towels from the dryer in the laundry room, hauled the basket into the family room and set them on Joel's recliner. Phoebe snatched the remote from the coffee table and powered on the television. Bluesie appeared, a blue cartoon dog that talked with an Australian accent.

"No, no, no. I said I want to watch the news. Channel 3, WTKR."

"I don't know how to change it."

"Yes, you do. Just press the number 3."

Phoebe screwed up her face and poked the button. When the channel changed, a middle-aged man with brown combed-back hair sat at a news desk and announced that a humpback whale washed up on the north end of Pea Island. A video of the huge creature displayed its carcass on the edge of the sea, waves slapping against it.

Phoebe's mouth dropped open, and her eyes grew wide. "Look, Mommy, another dead whale."

"That's the third one this year, and they all have been tangled up in nets. How sad."

Phoebe plopped down on the oak floor and stared at the screen.

*Maybe watching the news wasn't such a good idea.* Angie tugged several hand towels out of the basket and tossed them onto the couch. "Hey, Ladybug! Get over there and fold those towels."

Phoebe sat mesmerized.

"Hey, you! Fold those towels like I showed you."

Her focus broke from the television, and she stood and trudged to the couch. "Mommy, I feel so sorry for that whale."

Angie let out an exasperated breath. "I'll turn Bluesie back on." *A blue dog is better than a dead whale.* She pivoted and swiped the remote off the coffee table. When she turned toward the television, a color photograph of a red-haired girl with freckles appeared on the screen. *That's her! That's Kiara Bailey. They finally are letting the public know.*

The reporter said, "A seventeen-year-old Dare County girl, Kiara Bailey, has been missing for four days. Her parents informed local authorities that Kiara did not return home on Thursday evening. If you have seen Kiara or know anything of her whereabouts, please contact the Dare County Sheriff's Office."

*Did she run away?* Angie shook her head. *I don't even want to think of other possibilities. Last week Sammy said Stokes claimed he broke up with her. Breakups are traumatic for teenage girls, especially if the couple have been intimate.* She pressed the "last channel" button on the remote, and the blue dog cartwheeled across the screen.

Phoebe held up a folded hand towel. "Did you know that girl, Mommy?"

Angie took the towel. "I've seen her before."

"Is she lost?"

"I don't know, honey. Let's hope they find her soon." A loud knock startled her, and she almost dropped the remote. "Someone's at the door."

"I'll get it!" Phoebe charged through the family room and into the entry hall.

Angie heard the door open and the voice of a girl saying, "Hi, Phoebe." She stepped beyond the recliner so she could see who was there. Sammy Cline stood in the doorway. The black cat weaved between her ankles, rubbing its side against her shins.

"Hi Sammy," Phoebe said. "You brought Six Toes with you."

The cat strutted into the entry hall and meowed.

"I didn't bring him," Sammy said. "He was waiting on the porch when I got here." Her bright orange tank top and white shorts complimented her slim figure.

"Come on in, Sammy," Angie said. "Can you believe that cat walked here from Frisco? That's four miles. Male cats sure like to wander."

Sammy stepped into the house and closed the door. "You said I could come and talk to you if I needed to." Her voice shook slightly.

"Of course." Angie noticed a tenseness in her eyes. "Let's go into the kitchen, and I'll wrangle up some iced tea."

Phoebe led the way through the hall and into the kitchen. Midnight followed close at her feet.

Angie headed for the refrigerator. *I bet I know what this is all about.* "Have a seat, Sammy. I hope you like sweetened iced tea."

"That's fine." Sammy pulled out a chair and sat down.

Phoebe plopped down on the floor next to the dishwasher and stroked the cat's back. "I'll take milk, Mommy, and Six Toes wants a bowl of milk, too."

"His name is not Six Toes." Angie removed the pitcher of tea and milk carton from the fridge and closed the door. "His owner told us his name is Midnight." She set the containers on the counter, retrieved the glasses and bowl from the nearby cupboard and poured the drinks.

"I like that name." Phoebe rubbed the cat's cheeks. "It's midnight, and Midnight sits in the moonlight."

Angie smiled, recognizing the first line from one of Phoebe's favorite children's books. *I bet she has the whole book memorized.* She set the bowl next to the cat, handed Phoebe her cup of milk, went back to the counter for the glasses of tea and brought them to the table.

"I'm really worried about Kiara," Sammy said.

Angie sat across from her. "I thought maybe that's why you came here. We heard the bad news. When was the last time you saw her?"

"Wednesday afternoon. I wanted to ask her if she and John really broke up. She started to cry and said she was mad at John."

"So, they did break up?"

Sammy wobbled her head. "As far as Kiara is concerned. She said they had an argument. She missed her period, and John told her she better not be pregnant. She told me she was going to pick up a home pregnancy test. Later that night she called and said she saw two lines. It was positive."

"I wonder if she told Stokes."

"She did. He demanded that she get an abortion. That's when she realized he didn't love her or their baby. She didn't know what to do or where to go. She doesn't have a driver's license and didn't want to tell her parents about it."

"She needs to get counseling."

"I think it's too late. It's been four days, and no one has heard from her."

Angie nodded slowly. "That's true, but it might not be too late. She might be staying with friends or relatives. Maybe she found someone to take her to a clinic on the mainland and is recovering there."

Sammy frowned. "Maybe, but I have my doubts. She told me she would figure it out for herself and planned on breaking away from John and the gang."

"Do you think she ran away?"

Sammy shrugged. "Anything's possible. I've been thinking about something she told me that night. She said there are natural means of causing a miscarriage."

Angie straightened. "Like falling down steps?"

"No. She said there are special plants or roots you can eat."

"Where would she get them?"

"From the woman at the tree. A couple weeks ago we saw her collecting plants along the sound. Kiara said that Cora practices some kind of religion called Wicca. She has knowledge about natural cures and occult powers."

"Did she tell you she was going to visit Cora?"

"No, but the more I thought about it, the more sense it made. I wanted to see what you think."

"I think it's a good lead." Angie glanced at the cat and Phoebe. "I'll be paying her a visit tomorrow morning to return her cat again. I'll ask her."

Sammy took a deep breath. "Good. I tried to think like a detective. I was hoping my reasoning was good."

Angie raised a finger. "You'd make an excellent detective. In my business, you learn to turn over every stone."

Sammy gave a half smile. "I want to do everything I can to help find Kiara."

"I'll let my husband know about this. I'm sure the sheriff's department will want to question Cora, too."

Sammy stood. "Well, I better get home before it gets dark."

"I don't blame you. Walking alone in the dark isn't safe nowadays."

Sammy crossed the kitchen and knelt next to Phoebe and the cat. "It was nice to see you again, Phoebe."

Phoebe glanced up. "And Midnight, too?"

"Midnight, too. I like that name better than Six Toes."

"Me, too. It's the name of the cat in my favorite

book."

"What's the name of the book?" Sammy asked.

"*Moonlight and Midnight*. There's a crazy witch in the story, but her spells always go wrong."

Sammy took in a quick breath as if a jolt of static electricity zapped her. She glanced out the window at the darkening sky. "I've got to go."

# Chapter 9

The next morning Angie checked with Mee Mee to see if she wanted to tag along on the return visit to Cora's cabin. Mee Mee declared she was all in, so Angie picked her up at the bookstore at about quarter till eleven. As they headed down Route 12 through the mist of the overcast morning, Angie filled her in on Sammy's visit. She parked in the same spot along Old Doctors Road, and they got out of the Jeep.

The leaves, thickets and dwarf palmettos drooped with the weight of the dew and occasional drizzle. Their shoes left clear prints in the wet sand as they walked down the lane toward Pinecone Path. Even Midnight left paw prints as he led the way.

"I should have brought my raincoat," Mee Mee said. "It feels like a hard rain's a gonna fall."

"Sounds like a line from a sad song."

"It's a Dylan tune. There's a verse about walking through the middle of a sad forest."

Angie panned the surroundings. "I feel the vibe,

but Joel says it's going to clear up this afternoon."

"That's good to hear. Did you tell him that Kiara may have visited Cora?"

"Yeah. I'm sure they'll send someone out to question her."

"I guess we get first dibs."

"If we learn anything that matters, I'll call Joel and let him know."

When they turned onto Pinecone Path, the overhanging branches and thick foliage added another layer of darkness to the gloomy forest. The faint strains of a violin moaned through the trees. Mee Mee raised her eyebrows. "Sounds like a Stravinsky elegy."

"Or something you'd hear in a Hitchcock movie."

An owl hooted from deep in the woods, and the wind creaked the limbs of an old live oak near the path. The violin music seemed to grow sadder with every step. Midnight turned onto the trail that led to Cora's cabin. Angie peered through the tangled greenery and caught sight of the smoke that hovered above the moss-covered roof. She sniffed an odd odor. *Is that the smoke combined with the mustiness of the woods?*

When they neared the cabin, the music stopped. Mee Mee stepped up on the rough-hewn stoop to knock, but the door edged open before she got the chance. Cora gazed at them from the interior shadows. "I know why you are here." She opened the door wider, and Midnight entered the hovel. The same crimson dress hung on her medium frame.

"Your cat showed up on my porch again," Angie said.

"Yes, but you've come to talk about the girl who visited me. Please come in and sit down."

Angie raised and lowered her chin. *There she goes again with her gnostic knowledge.* They entered and took the same seats where they sat last week at the round table. Cora eased herself onto the chair across from her, and Angie said, "Kiara Bailey visited you?"

"She didn't tell me her name. She had long red hair and freckles, maybe seventeen or eighteen years old."

"That's the girl." Angie leaned forward. "Did you know her parents reported her missing?"

Cora put her hand to her chest. "When she left, I felt a heaviness deep within my heart. She was a very troubled girl. I feared something might happen to her."

"It's been four days and no sign of her." Angie said.

"She came here on Thursday afternoon." Cora took a deep breath. "She wanted me to give her something to abort her unborn child."

Mee Mee glanced around the cabin at the shelves crowded with jars of plants and roots. "Do you have something here that could do that?"

Cora bobbed her head slowly. "Mugwort. It's a plant that can be used as an herbal medicine to improve sleep. It's also been known to help irregular menstrual cycles. A high dosage of the plant, though, can induce contractions that can cause a miscarriage."

Angie lowered her head and bored her eyes into the

woman. "Did you give her that plant?"

"No. I swear I didn't."

"Did you give her anything?" Mee Mee asked.

She shook her head. "I told her I couldn't help her. She begged me to give her something that would end her pregnancy, but I told her she needed to talk to a doctor. I didn't want to take the chance."

Mee Mee tilted her head. "What do you mean?"

"Miscarriages can be dangerous. If anything happened to her, I would get the blame. Now I have two reasons to be worried."

Angie's eyes narrowed. "Two reasons?"

Cora nodded. "I'm worried about the girl. She was desperate. Desperate people make bad choices."

"What else?" Mee Mee asked.

She stared at the door, eyes tensing. "If something happened to her, they'll come after me."

"Who will come after you?" Angie said.

"Those who fear me and my way of life. People who jump to conclusions. The past is a circle that repeats itself."

Angie shifted in her chair and straightened. "I hope you realize that the local authorities will want to question you about Kiara's visit?"

"I have nothing to hide. If questioning me will help them find the girl, I'll tell them everything I told you."

"Good." Angie rested her hands on the table. "You never know what information may lead to a break in a missing person's case."

Cora frowned, lowered her head and stared

sullenly at her lap.

"What's the matter? Are you okay?" Mee Mee asked.

"I saw something else."

"Something that could help find Kiara?" Angie asked.

Cora shut her eyes. "It might somehow be connected."

Mee Mee touched her shoulder. "What did you see?"

Her eyes opened and focused on the ceiling. "When I was at the tree a few days ago, I had a vision. I saw a young man on the top of a tall tower. The sun was high in the sky. Another man handed him a small package. There was a word written on the package."

"Could you make out the word?" Mee Mee said.

"The word was *DEATH*."

Angie bit her lip. *Here we go with the psychic stuff again.* "What do you think your vision means?"

"I'm not sure, but early this morning I awakened to the same dream—the tower and the men. Today must be the day when this happens."

"Did you recognize either of the men?" Mee Mee asked.

"The one who appeared first on the tower was the young man who threatened me at the tree."

"John Stokes," Angie recalled.

"I believe that is his name. I know he and the girl are romantically involved. I've seen them holding hands on my morning walks."

"So, you think Stokes has something to do with her disappearance?"

She met Angie's stare. "I've gazed into the pit of his soul. He is a pawn in their game, and Algol is their king. His fealty to their reign of ruin serves to drag young people into the depths of darkness."

Mee Mee blinked several times and eyed Angie. "Okay . . . that was an interesting way to put it."

Angie's lips tightened into a thin line as she shifted her attention from Mee Mee to Cora. "I'm not sure what all that means, but obviously, you think John Stokes knows something."

Cora's left eye closed halfway. "He is the one the authorities should question."

Angie scooted out her chair and stood. "I'm sure they will if they haven't already. We've got to go." She checked her watch. "I need to be somewhere soon."

An odd half-smile formed on Cora's face. "I understand."

Mee Mee stood and straightened her nylon jacket. "Thank you for welcoming us again. Let's hope Kiara Bailey shows up sometime today." She took a deep breath and let it out. "That would be the best outcome for everyone."

Cora folded her hands on the tabletop. "Hope does not always determine outcomes."

"True," Mee Mee said, "but it doesn't hurt."

As Angie walked toward the door, she saw Midnight stretched out on a small throw rug. "I hope your cat has nine lives. He sure travels these busy roads between here and Buxton."

"Midnight is free to wander. He always comes back to me."

Angie forced a smile. *Yeah, thanks to me.* "It's been real . . . interesting." She opened the door and walked outside. Mee Mee followed, waving and bidding goodbye to Cora.

Mee Mee closed the door and said, "Did you get all that?"

Angie put some distance between herself and the cabin before she answered. "Not really. It was very cryptic. I'd like to know who King Algol is."

"I can Google that." As they walked along the path Mee Mee slipped her phone out of her jacket pocket, activated it and entered the inquiry. "Says here that Algol is the demon of drugs and alcohol. His goal is to drag human beings into his world of darkness."

"Makes sense. Cora knows what's going on."

"It says that Algol is one of the most powerful and dangerous demons. The souls of this world who abuse drugs are under his control."

"And Cora wants us to do something about it."

"What makes you say that?"

Angie turned onto the Pinecone Path. "Her vision of the tower."

"Go on."

"I believe that vision was stirred by a message she discovered in the hole of the Cora Tree. She examined it and put it back where she found it. John Stokes retrieved that message, and Sammy Cline glimpsed it before he tucked it away."

"What was on it?"

"The drawing of a tower, some words and the numbers 1245. Sammy couldn't make out the words, but I'm guessing there was a date on it."

Mee Mee funneled the phone back into her pocket. "So, Cora saw the note, read the words and somehow surmised that a drug deal was about to go down sometime today."

"Right. People who know about the legend leave notes and trinkets in the hole of the tree. Stopping there and looking into the hole wouldn't be considered unusual. It could be a contact point for Stokes's supplier."

"Why didn't she just come out and tell us?"

"She wants us to think she has paranormal powers. I thought maybe she did, but now I have my doubts."

They reached the sandy lane, and Mee Mee said, "Perhaps she wants the townspeople to know she's not the Wicked Witch of the West. She's more like the other one. What's her name?"

"Glenda."

"Right. She wants to show up out of nowhere and save the day."

"Uh huh. Helping to put the bad guys behind bars would turn her into a clairvoyant crusader. That would go a long way to improve her reputation in the public's eye." They approached the car and Angie dug into her jeans pocket for her key fob. "Are you in a hurry to get back to the bookstore?"

"Dreary days are busy days. I better get back."

"Okay. I'll drop you off on the way." Angie opened the door and climbed into the Jeep.

Mee Mee scurried around the front end, threw open the door and plopped onto the passenger seat. "On the way? Where are you going in such a hurry?"

"To the only tower on this island."

"The Cape Hatteras Lighthouse?"

"Correct." Angie checked her watch. "It's half past eleven. Cora said the sun was high in the sky when the two men met on the tower."

"What are you going to do there?"

"Wait and watch."

"A stakeout?"

Angie grinned. "You could call it that."

"I'm all in. Kathy can handle the store."

Angie started the Gladiator. "Let's go."

# Chapter 10

As Angie turned onto Lighthouse Road, the clouds transitioned to lighter shades of gray with blue patches appearing and separating the hazy masses. Sunlight broke through and brightened the tall bushes and brambles that lined the sides of the road. Rounding a long curve, Angie spied the top half of the spiral-striped spire towering above a row of pines, swamp bay and wax myrtle trees.

"Do you think Stokes will show up?" Mee Mee asked.

"Hard to say. This might be a wild goose chase. We're basing our expedition on a crude sketch and a crystal ball gazer's fancy. However, there is an interesting detail that may add some prospect to this snipe hunt."

"What's that?"

"The numbers that Sammy saw on the message: 1245. What do you think they mean?"

Mee Mee scratched her chin. "I'll go with a simple

explanation: a quarter to one in the afternoon—12:45."

"My thoughts exactly. If you are going to meet someone, you better give them a time and a place."

Angie made a left onto the road that led to the parking lot and pulled in next to a black Subaru Impreza. She scanned the area and saw a covered shelter with a good view of the lighthouse entrance. As she stepped out of the car, she said, "Just act like a tourist and don't stare at anyone who might look suspicious."

"Don't worry. I got this." Mee Mee exited the Jeep and caught up with Angie.

They walked across a cement promenade and up a wide wooden ramp next to a hipped-roofed outbuilding. The Hatteras Island Visitor's Center was to the right, but they made a left onto the wooden walkway that led to the shelter. They sat on a bench stationed along the railing in the far corner of the shelter.

Angie checked her watch. "It's a few minutes to twelve. We may be sitting here for an hour before anything happens."

"Good. I need to do something." Mee Mee stood.

"Where are you going?"

"To the little girl's room. Just relax. Keep your eyes peeled. I'll be back in a few minutes." She strolled across the wooden walkway toward the Visitor Center.

*I need to go, too.* She studied the fifteen or so people who meandered in front of the lighthouse. They all looked like tourists, dressed in colorful tops, shorts, wide hats and sunglasses. *I can hold it.* She chuckled to herself. *Detective work demands the endurance of the human bladder.*

As the minutes passed the urgency increased. Finally, Mee Mee returned and sat next to her. "Feel better?" Angie said.

"I'm doing better than a one-legged cat in a sandbox."

"Good, because I've got to go now. I haven't seen anyone who looks suspicious. Keep checking on the people hanging out by the lighthouse entrance. I'll be back in a few minutes."

"I'm on it like a seagull on a French fry."

Angie shook her head, stood and hurried to the Visitor Center. Once inside, she noticed a couple families with young children but didn't see anyone who looked like they were about to hand John Stokes a death package. She entered the restroom and took care of her business. Leaving the Visitor Center, she felt more relaxed. *Whew! My bladder was about to blow a gasket. Hopefully, nothing happened while I was gone.*

As she approached the shelter, she caught sight of Mee Mee staring intently in the direction of the lighthouse. She sat down next to her. "Notice something unusual?

"Those two Hispanic guys."

Angie peered toward the redbrick base of the spire and saw a short guy, maybe five feet six inches in height, and a tall, thin man with medium length black hair and a thin mustache. The shorter guy was stocky with a shaved head and full black beard. They both wore jeans and long-sleeved, light-colored lapel shirts. They had rolled their sleeves up to just below their elbows.

"What about them?"

"They were in the Visitor Center. I noticed tattoos on their necks and the exposed parts of their arms. One of them purchased a ticket to climb to the top of the lighthouse."

"They might be local workers. A lot of Mexicans work for the landscape companies."

"I'm aware of that, but I Googled their tattoos. Look at this." She held up her phone. A closeup of a tattooed forearm appeared on the screen: a feminine-looking skeleton wearing a saintly hooded robe and clasping a rosary. Skulls were piled at her feet.

"That is gruesome."

"It's a common cartel tattoo known as Santa Muerte or the Lady of Holy Death. By honoring Santa Muerte and the dead, the gang member receives protection despite the evil he has committed."

Angie could feel her heart ramp up. "Which one bought the ticket?"

"The short one."

"He's just standing there."

"Must not be in any hurry to climb the spiral staircase to the sky."

Angie nodded slowly. "He's waiting for somebody." Angie grasped her arm and whispered,

"Look away. The short one's staring right at you."

Mee Mee shifted on the bench and redirected her eyes to the parking lot. "I wonder which car is theirs?"

"Hard to say. They arrived before us." Angie glanced back at the muscular guy. He gazed in their direction. She turned and inspected the parking lot. "He's still looking at us," she said in a low voice.

Mee Mee patted her knee. "We're just a couple tourists."

"Yeah, we're on a road trip alright." Angie huffed in a quick breath. "There he is—John Stokes. He's walking toward the ramp that leads to the Visitor Center."

"Is he the tall kid wearing black cargo shorts and an orange tank top?"

"Yes, Ma'am." Angie watched him trot up the ramp and cross the walkway. "I bet he's going to go get a ticket to climb to the top of the tower."

"There he goes into the Visitor Center."

"We'll just sit tight and see what happens."

A few minutes passed as they eyed the door to the Visitor Center, not saying much. Stokes exited the building, turned right and descended the steps to the path that wound its way through a stand of trees toward the lighthouse. He disappeared behind the greenery, and Angie turned about ninety degrees to her left to check out the two guys at the base of the tower. They stared in the direction of the path.

"There he is," Mee Mee murmured.

Stokes walked straight down the sidewalk to the

lighthouse entrance, glancing and nodding at the two men. He handed the attendant the ticket and entered.

Angie checked her watch. "It's twenty-five minutes to one. He's ten minutes early."

"Early is good unless you're a mouse."

"What?"

Mee Mee smirked and withdrew something out of her jacket pocket. "The second mouse gets the cheese."

"Is that what I think it is?"

Mee Mee nodded. "After I saw the short guy buy a ticket, I got in line. I'm climbing the spiral staircase to the sky."

"That's not a good idea."

"Why not? It's open to the public."

Angie tapped her chest. "I've got a bad feeling about it."

"I'll be careful. Besides, from up there I might see or hear something important. Remember, a girl's life is at stake."

Angie grimaced. "That's true, but they already suspect we've been checking them out."

"There he goes. The short one is heading to the entrance." She stood.

"Mee Mee, please don't do this."

She waved her off. "I'm just a tourist on a road trip." She pointed to the top of the lighthouse. "And that's the most famous lighthouse in the world." She pivoted and headed down the walkway.

*Son of a biscuit eater. Keep calm. Don't draw attention to yourself.* She took a deep breath. *Doesn't she realize how dangerous these cartel thugs are?* Several minutes passed. Angie got to her feet. *I need to find a spot where I can clearly see what's going on.* She hurried down the walkway, turned left past the Visitor Center and descended to the path. Walking in the shade of the trees, she tried to relax and control her breathing. At the edge of the trees, she stopped and stood where the tall man couldn't catch sight of her. *I can see the catwalk from here. There's Stokes, coming out the door. He's walking to the railing.*

She inspected her surroundings but didn't see anyone who took notice of her. A few minutes later the short guy with the beard stepped onto the catwalk and circled to where Stokes leaned against the railing. Less than a minute passed before Mee Mee emerged from the doorway. *Wow. She flew up those steps. That's a workout.* She edged along the curved wall and stopped about ten feet from Stokes and the short guy. Tilting her head slightly, she bent her right ear, as if she was scratching it, towards the men.

Angie blinked several times to clear her vision. *Mee Mee, you're living dangerously.* From her viewpoint she had no idea what kind of interaction Stokes and the short guy were having. *Friendly talk? I doubt it. He's probably telling Stokes not to screw up, or they'd pry his fingernails off. Maybe Mee Mee is catching some of their words.* Another minute passed, and the short guy patted Stokes's back and turned. Mee Mee dropped her hand just in time. As he walked by Mee Mee, he hesitated and gave her the once over. She nodded toward him. He kept his eyes on her as he headed to the door but then shifted his focus to the doorway as he entered the lighthouse.

Stokes remained at the railing. *He's giving them a chance to put some distance between them. Come on, Mee Mee, don't let Stokes see you, too.* Mee Mee traipsed back to the main gallery door. *Good. She's coming down.* Three minutes later the short guy emerged from the base and walked to where the tall one stood. Angie stayed in the shadows of the trees but could watch them through the breaks in the leaves.

A minute later Mee Mee appeared in the doorway, descended the few steps and strode down the sidewalk toward the trees. *Step on it!* As she neared, Mee Mee eyed her and winked. With both hands Angie raked her fingers through her pixie-cut hair, her jaw tensing. *This ain't no frolic in the park.* "Come on," Angie urged under her breath. She clasped Mee Mee's hand and tugged her along the path toward the Visitor Center.

"What's the hurry?"

"I want to get to the car before the two cartel guys see us."

"Okay."

Angie let go of her hand. "The short guy got a good look at you."

"Sorry about that. He turned around before I could walk away."

"You can't mess around with these guys. They're natural born killers."

"Don't you think I look fairly harmless?"

"He eyed you like he saw a rattlesnake."

They rushed across the walkway, down the ramp and into the parking lot. At the car they split apart, threw open the doors and darted inside. As Angie caught her breath she gave Mee Mee the stink eye.

"What? I overheard some important details."

"Like what?"

"First of all, I saw the exchange. It was a package about the size of a beanbag."

"So, we know what we assumed: Stokes is a dealer for a Mexican cartel."

Mee Mee raised a finger. "That's not all. I heard the short guy say that the boss will be arriving at the house soon."

"Hmmmm." Angie creased her brow. "Joel said they may have a headquarters established in Hatteras or Frisco. Sounds like a big fish in the organization may show up there. Did he say where?"

"No, but I heard something else. He told Stokes not to worry about the problem with his girlfriend."

"I wonder what he meant by that?"

Mee Mee shrugged. "Her pregnancy?"

"Maybe." Angie peered through the windshield. "Here they come."

"They're walking right towards us."

Angie looked through the passenger window. "That black Impreza might be theirs."

As the short guy cut between the two vehicles, he hesitated before opening the door, glancing in their direction. Mee Mee abruptly turned and faced Angie, her eyes wide as silver dollars. He squinted at the window but then clambered into the car, slammed the door and started the engine. Angie gazed at her rearview mirror and watched them back out and pull away toward the exit.

She started the Gladiator. "I hate to say this, but we've got to follow them."

"If Kiara is in that house with the Big Fish, . . ."

"Then we need to find out where that house is."

# Chapter 11

Angie drove out of the parking lot and around the first turn. A couple hundred yards ahead, she saw the Impreza make a right at the stop sign. "They're heading back to Route 12."

"Do you think they'll drive to the house the short guy mentioned?"

"I hope so. If we can track them to their headquarters, Joel and his taskforce can execute a search warrant."

"That would be good gravy on homemade biscuits, especially if they find Kiara there."

Angie kept her distance for the next mile along Lighthouse Road. When the Impreza reached the stop sign, she hit her brakes and slowed until the black car turned left on Route 12. Then she accelerated to catch up.

"They're heading south through Buxton," Mee Mee said. "I hope we don't lose them."

A blue Chevy Suburban sailed by before Angie

reached the stop sign, but she quickly turned onto Route 12 and caught up with the SUV. The large vehicle made it difficult to see the Impreza. A couple kids wearing ballcaps turned and waved at her through the back window. The left blinker flashed, and the Suburban turned into the parking lot of Burrus Field, a youth baseball facility. The Impreza was only thirty yards ahead. Angie hit the brakes and backed off another twenty yards.

A quarter mile down the road the Impreza slowed, its brake lights glowing. *Are they stopping at Conner's Market?* Angie applied her brakes to keep from getting too close. Their left turn signal kicked on.

"That's the Cape Pines Motel up ahead on the left," Mee Mee said. "Do you think they're staying there?"

"I don't know. That's not a house." Angie watched the Impreza turn into the motel's lot, but it didn't park in front of one of the rooms. The car circled around the pool toward the exit and came to a stop in the grass near the main road. "Don't look at them." Angie drove by the motel gazing straight ahead. She made a right into the United Bank lot and pulled into a space where they could observe the black car from a distance.

Mee Mee leaned against the dashboard. "Why did they park off to the side?"

"I don't think they're staying there."

"Are they watching us?"

"Possibly. Maybe they're being cautious, waiting to see if we're really bank customers."

Mee Mee said, "I'll get out and walk into the bank.

Hopefully, that will convince them."

Before Angie could respond, Mee Mee popped open the door, stepped out of the Jeep and marched toward the bank.

The two men remained in the car. *I hope the short guy doesn't recognize her. They're not budging. No way are they staying at the Cape Pines Motel.* Angie turned and eyed the bank entrance. The seconds passed more slowly than a turtle climbing a sand dune. Finally, Mee Mee exited the bank, hurried to the Jeep and got in.

"What's happening?"

"They're waiting for us to make the next move." Angie put the Jeep in reverse. "We can't stay here, or they'll know for sure we're trailing them." She backed the car up, shifted into drive and headed south on Route 12.

Mee Mee twisted in her seat and peered out the back window. "Now they're following us."

"I was afraid of that." Angie checked her rearview mirror. "At least they're not tailgating us." *What do I do now? Call Joel?*

"My bookstore is up around the next turn. Are you dropping me off?"

"No way. I don't want them to know where you work. These cartel guys are coldblooded."

"Thanks. I don't want to end up like the family in Capote's book."

"Huh?"

"Never mind. Keep driving."

"I'm turning down Crossway Road. We'll see what they do." Angie turned left onto the country lane.

Mee Mee checked the back window. "They're still tailing us."

Angie glanced at the rearview mirror. The Impreza remained about forty yards back. *I hope I didn't just make a judgment error. There're aren't many houses along these back roads.* The narrow lane weaved like a black snake through the greenery and then passed a trailer park.

"That's Buxton Back Road up ahead at the stop sign," Mee Mee said.

"Good name for it."

"You can turn right toward Frisco or make a left and head back to the north end of Buxton."

Angie slowed but didn't stop at the sign and turned left. "We're heading back to Buxton, . . ." She checked the rearview mirror. ". . . and so are they."

"Maybe they're just trying to scare us."

"Yeah, they're professional intimidators."

"At least they're not ramming the back of your Jeep."

"Not yet." Angie patted the steering wheel. "I'd put my money on the Gladiator any day. Get my Beretta out of the console, just in case we need it."

"Okay." Mee Mee triggered the latch, raised the cover, reached in and pulled the handgun out of the console. "Whew! That's a black beauty."

"Do you know how to use it?"

"Sure, but I'll let you do the honors."

"Keep it handy. Route 12 is up ahead. We're going in circles." Angie stopped, checked both ways and turned left onto the highway. They passed a gas station on the left and a Dollar Store on the right. The Impreza stayed with them.

"Look! Up ahead!" Mee Mee said. "That's a sheriff's car coming this way."

"That might be Joel. He's turning into the Osprey Shopping Center. He eats lunch at the Buxton Munch Company." Angie flicked on her left turn signal as the white patrol car headed down the driveway toward the shopping center. She sped up, turned into the shopping center entrance and caught up with the Crown Victoria.

Mee Mee checked the back window. "They slowed down, but they're not following us. There they go. They're speeding away."

"They know better. They may be dangerous, but they're not stupid." Angie parked on the right side of the cruiser in front of the restaurant. "You can put the gun back where you got it."

"Maybe later, Black Beauty." Mee Mee opened the console and deposited the gun.

When Angie stepped out of the car, she took a deep breath and let it out.

Joel circled the front of the Crown Victoria and planted his hands on his hips. "What are you doing here? Stalking me?"

"I bet you say that to all the girls." Angie motioned toward the entrance. "Let's get something to eat, and

I'll tell you all about it."

# Chapter 12

The Buxton Munch Company was a great place to get wraps and burgers. Although it was a small restaurant, it was by far the most colorful one in the area. Its walls, painted lime green, bright yellow, orange and azure blue, were decorated with seascapes, plastic crabs, flipflops and wooden fish cutouts. Joel led them to a table below a painting of the Cape Hatteras Lighthouse.

They took their seats, and Joel eyed Angie. "You look a little stressed."

Angie raised her eyebrows. "A little? You don't know how relieved I was to see you turn in here."

"Hunger pains can make you jump out of your skin."

Angie wagged her head. "Hunger had nothing to do with it."

"We were on a stakeout," Mee Mee said. "We saw a drug deal go down."

Joel straightened and braced his hands on the table.

"Are you serious?"

Angie nodded. "Two guys from a Mexican cartel and John Stokes."

A willowy middle-aged brunette with a ponytail approached their table and took their orders. Joel went for the Swiss mushroom burger, fries and coffee. Both Angie and Mee Mee ordered chicken wraps and iced tea.

Once the waitress departed, Joel asked, "How do you know they were cartel members?"

Mee Mee raised a finger. "I identified their *Holy Lady of Death* tattoos."

Joel gave Mee Mee a doubletake. "Tim Shepherd, my contact with the DEA, showed me some images of that tattoo along with several others. Where did the deal take place?"

Mee Mee pointed to the painting above them.

"The Cape Hatteras Lighthouse?"

Mee Mee nodded. "One of them handed Stokes a small package."

Angie raised her hand shoulder high. "Let me start from the beginning." She lowered her hand and recounted their interaction with Cora and the new information about Kiara Bailey's visit. She reiterated Cora's vision of the tower and the possibility that she found the same message that John Stokes retrieved from the tree. Angie tapped the table twice and said, "Then she doubled down by telling us she had the same dream about the tower this morning. She was convinced the exchange would take place today."

"Sounds like Cora wanted you to stakeout the lighthouse," Joel said.

Angie agreed. "I don't know if she really has paranormal powers, but she obviously knows what's going on with John Stokes."

"Maybe Stokes is her poison ivy in the petunia patch," Mee Mee said. "She came to Frisco to commune with the past, and he wants her banned from the tree's portal."

"Right." Joel brushed his knuckles against the bristle on his jawline. "Get Stokes arrested, and she can visit the Cora Tree hassle free."

"Anyway, we headed to the lighthouse and set up camp in a nearby shelter. Two Hispanic guys were hanging out at the base." Angie thumbed toward Mee Mee. "Then Nancy Drew here went off the chain on me."

Joel shifted his eyes to Mee Mee. "Off the chain?"

A guilty grin lifted the corners of her mouth. "I followed Stokes and one of the cartel boys to the top of the lighthouse."

Joel shook his head. "That move could come back to haunt you."

"It did," Angie said. "What she heard up there forced our hand."

Mee Mee's eyes widened. "They mentioned a house and told Stokes not to worry about his girlfriend. We figured they might be keeping her at that house."

"So, I felt obligated to tail them. I was hoping we

could locate their headquarters. Then you and your team could execute a search warrant."

Joel nodded. "And rescue Kiara Bailey."

"And arrest the Big Fish," Mee Mee added.

Joel tilted his head, a quizzical look in his eyes.

"I heard him say that the boss was at the house."

"Now that would be a catch," Joel said.

"Don't get too excited," Angie grumbled. "We followed them to the Cape Pines Motel, but they caught on to us. We parked at the bank lot across the street. They just sat there in their car. Finally, we left, and the tables turned."

"They followed you."

"Right," Angie said. "We turned off on Crossway Road and circled back."

Mee Mee said, "When the bad boys spotted your cruiser, they took off. I guess we should thank your hankering for a Swiss mushroom burger."

Joel offered a half smile. "I didn't fight my way to the top of the food chain to become a vegetarian. Did you get the make of the car and license plate?"

Angie nodded. "A black Subaru Impreza with a Texas rental plate on it. I can't remember the numbers."

"How'd you know it was a rental?" Mee Mee asked.

"I noticed the license plate frame and sticker next to it. I'm sure they gave false info to rent the vehicle."

"True," Joel said, "but I bet there's not many black Imprezas cruising the island. I'll alert our dispatcher and tell him to spread the word."

A few minutes later the brunette returned with a trayful of food. Smiling warmly, she distributed the meals and drinks. "Can I get you anything else?"

"I'm smug as a clam in high water," Mee Mee said.

Joel said, "We're good."

"I'll check back in a few." She about faced and returned to the counter.

They spent the next fifteen minutes devouring their lunch. In between bites Angie provided a detailed description of the cartel thugs. Joel was anxious to share all the new leads with Agent Shepherd and put a tail on Stokes now that they were sure he was a dealer.

"I wish we could have located the house," Mee Mee lamented, "for Kiara's sake."

"Being Stokes's girlfriend," Angie said, "she probably knows too much. These cartels are notorious for human trafficking. That poor girl is pregnant. We need to find that house."

Mee Mee's eyes glazed over. "Before it's too late."

"At least we know the make and color of their car," Joel said. "I'll tell our officers about the girl. Hopefully, someone will spot the vehicle parked in front of a house. Then we'll check to see if the car has Texas rental plates. Because the girl's life is in danger, we can make a warrantless entry."

"Good," Angie sighed. "Maybe our efforts won't be wasted."

Mee Mee let out a low whistle. "The sooner you nail

them the better. I don't like being on those thugs' radar."

"You two need to grow eyes in the back of your head." Joel's two-way radio buzzed, and he snatched it from his belt. "Deputy Thomas Here." His eyebrows tensed, the space between them narrowing. "Can you give me a more definite location?" He nodded several times. "Got it. I'll be there in a few minutes."

"What's up?" Angie asked.

"Someone called in an anonymous tip about a body in the Buxton Woods. Deputy Charlton checked it out and found the remains. He's at the scene waiting for the E-squad."

"Who is it?" Angie asked.

"Don't know yet."

Mee Mee's brown eyes seemed to darken. "Did he say where in the woods?"

"Yeah. Not far off a trail called the Pinecone Path. I'm going there now."

Angie shot up, her chair almost tipping over. "So are we."

# Chapter 13

Angie followed Joel's cruiser to Old Doctors Road. The memory of the odd smell she had detected on that morning's visit to Cora's cabin triggered an olfactory revulsion. *I should have known it was the smell of death.*

"Who do you think it is?" Mee Mee asked. "Cora?"

"Could be, but I doubt it. I noticed an odor when we approached the cabin. I thought it was the smell of the woods and smoke from Cora's stove. Now I'm thinking it must have been decomposition from a body nearby."

"It wasn't near the path, or we would have seen it."

"We don't know much yet. Lots of people walk through these woods. Some old guy may have had a heart attack, stumbled through the trees and keeled over."

"That's possible. Or maybe someone committed a murder and dug a shallow grave. On the crime shows they always find the body in a shallow grave."

"Let's not let our imaginations get too carried

away."

"Mine's in high gear right now. I've got a bad feeling about this."

*Me, too.* Angie tried to relax her breathing. After driving a couple hundred yards down Old Doctors Road, she noticed red flashing lights through the foliage. "The E-Squad is here already. You might want to wait in the car. Seeing a dead body can be unnerving, especially if it's a bloody crime scene."

"I'll be fine. You'd be surprised at what I've seen during my lifetime."

"You *are* full of surprises."

Joel stopped the Crown Victoria about twenty feet behind the red emergency vehicle, and Angie pulled in behind him. Another cruiser, lights flashing, was parked in front of the E-squad. They got out of the Jeep, hurried along the sandy lane to the Pinecone Path and caught up with Joel.

Angie pointed down the trail. "Cora's cabin is about a quarter mile from here."

Joel said, "Maybe she saw or heard something."

"I hope she's still okay," Mee Mee fretted. "Remember, those teenage boys were out to get her."

They approached the narrow path that turned off toward Cora's cabin. Angie spotted people through the breaks between the trees and bushes about forty yards to their left. "There they are. We'll have to cut through the woods to get there."

Pushing branches out of her way, Angie led them past trees and around shrubbery until they entered a small clearing. Three emergency crew members and Deputy Charlton, a young guy with a bulbous nose and pockmarked cheeks, stared at the body. When Angie got a clear view, she recognized the matted red hair and freckles spattering the girl's gray complexion—Kiara Bailey. Her lifeless eyes stared upwards beyond the canopy of branches where a thick cloud blotted the sun. The morning drizzle had soaked her white V-neck tank top and blue jeans, tattered with fashionable holes. Wet weeds draped over her outstretched arms and legs. Flies buzzed above her face. The smell turned Angie's stomach.

Angie swallowed a knot in her throat and leaned on her knees. "That's Kiara Bailey."

"Don't disturb anything," Deputy Charlton warned. "We're waiting for the CSI guys to get here. Could be murder. Could be suicide. We don't know."

"Poor girl," Mee Mee's voice faltered, and she took in a few long, slow breaths. "A young person's death is a terrible thing."

Joel circled to the other side of the clearing, keeping his distance from the body. Turning, he faced the woods in the direction of the cabin and examined the ground.

*What's he doing? Probably looking for footprints.* Angie shifted her focus to the girl's neck. *No bruises.* She scrutinized the rest of her body as best she could from where she stood. *Don't see any marks on her wrists or arms. No contusions on her face. Maybe she overdosed because of her pregnancy?* Angie cleared her throat and coughed. "There may be more than one person who died here."

Deputy Charlton looked askance at her. "I don't think so. I checked the area thoroughly."

"We got word that she may be pregnant." Angie said.

"Ohhhh, I see." He tilted his head and raised an eyebrow. "That's an important detail. Could be a motive."

"For murder or suicide?" Mee Mee asked.

"Either," Deputy Charlton said.

Joel walked back to where Angie and Mee Mee stood. "There's an overgrown path back there that leads to the cabin. She may have come from that direction."

Deputy Charlton pointed toward the Pinecone Path. "Here comes the CSI team. He faced the EMS crew. "It'll be a while before you boys collect the body."

"We'll keep out of the way," the tall one said. The other two murmured and nodded.

A short man, probably in his mid-fifties, emerged from behind a thicket. Smoking a cigar, he wore a black fedora and a shabby rain jacket. His wrinkled shirt and disheveled tie looked like they had been extracted from an overloaded laundry basket. Two guys wearing black Polo shirts followed him, one had a thick mustache and the other carried a camera.

With his thumb and forefinger, the short man withdrew the cigar from his mouth. As he approached, he said, "Greetings and salutations. I'm Detective Claudio. What do we have here?" His voice was gravelly.

Deputy Charlton updated him on the anonymous call and the discovery of the body. He noted that Angie had identified the girl as Kiara Bailey and reported on the possibility of her pregnancy.

Claudio eyed Angie. "Did you know her?"

"I knew of her. Her best friend is my neighbor."

"How old was she?"

"Seventeen or eighteen."

"Now that's interesting." Claudio edged closer to the body, planted his hands on his knees and leaned forward. "Why would a teenager be walking through these woods? Kids don't go on hikes nowadays for the fun of it. There must be a reason."

*Should I tell him about Cora? I can't withhold information.* Angie cleared her throat. "We know that she visited a woman who lives in a cabin over there." She turned and pointed toward the hovel.

He straightened, narrowed one eye and peered in the direction of the cabin. "How long ago did she make the visit?"

"About four days ago."

"Do you know why?"

"She was desperate. She thought the woman might be able to help her."

"Help her?" He closed one eye, tilted his head and stuck the cigar back in the corner of his mouth. He pivoted and motioned at his two assistants. "Jones, put up the crime tape. Burns, you can start taking photographs." The cigar flipped up and down with every word. He faced the onlookers and withdrew the cigar. "I'm sorry, but you people are going to have to back up about thirty yards. Watch where you step."

Joel sidled up to him as the others backed away from the body. "Detective Claudio, I'm Deputy Joel Thomas."

"I've seen you around."

"I'm heading up a drug taskforce for the Dare County Sheriff's Office. Do you mind if I head over to that cabin and interview the occupant? I'll report right back to you."

Claudio blew out a jet of gray smoke. "Not at all. Tell her not to go anywhere. I'll be coming that way in about a half hour to follow up."

"Will do." Joel walked to the outskirts of the clearing. He made eye contact with Angie and pointed to the other side where he had located the overgrown path to the cabin.

Angie nodded and high stepped through the weeds toward the path. Mee Mee kept pace a few steps behind her.

Joel took the lead and plodded along the overgrown path, checking the ground and weeds to detect any kind of disturbance. "I don't see any footprints. Of course, the rain over the last two days may have washed them away."

"Why did you mention Kiara's visit to Cora's cabin?" Mee Mee complained. "That detective will figure she's a prime suspect."

"She is a prime suspect," Angie said.

"You don't believe that do you?"

"It doesn't matter what I believe. We know that Kiara visited her to ask for a natural way to abort her baby."

"But Cora told us she didn't give her anything."

Angie halted, turned and faced Mee Mee. "And maybe that's true, but we don't know for sure. Let's hope the autopsy evidence clears Cora of any wrongdoing."

Mee Mee wagged her head. "If word gets out that she's a suspect, many people in this town will assume her guilt is a foregone conclusion."

Joel backtracked and stepped up to them. "That would be a shame, but this isn't the 1700s. I don't think anyone will go on a witch hunt and burn her at the stake."

Mee Mee glanced back at the clearing where Detective Claudio puffed away on his cigar while the photographer snapped photos. "I wouldn't be so sure about that."

Joel turned and continued down the path. "Come on. Let's go see what she has to say."

As they approached the cabin, Angie spotted Midnight on the stoop near the half-open door. The cat let out a long, mournful bellow.

"Cora!" Mee Mee called through the opening. "Cora, are you in there?" She stepped onto the stoop, pushed the door wide open and panned the room.

"She's not here." She entered the cabin and peered into the dark corners.

Angie and Joel stepped inside, and Midnight followed them. The violin and bow leaned against the back of a wooden chair near an open window. The sound of burning wood crackled from the stove. Midnight gazed up at Angie and bawled again. Joel walked around the perimeter of the room and stopped to inspect two rows of shelves crowded with jars containing specimens and plants.

Mee Mee paced to the back and checked out the stove. "She has water on the boil over here." She grasped the handle, lifted the pot and set it on a nearby counter.

"She left in a hurry," Angie said.

Joel lifted a jar from one of the shelves and held it in the shaft of light from the window. "Interesting. Long, pointy green leaves with little spikes."

Mee Mee drifted toward him. "That looks like aloe vera. Its juices can treat skin ailments and bee stings. Cora is an expert in medicinal plants."

Angie walked to the window near the chair and violin. "This window is facing the clearing where Kiara's body was found." She took a long whiff. "I can smell the decomposition. Cora probably heard the sirens. She may have walked into the woods to see what was happening."

Midnight leapt onto the round table in the middle of the room. The cat meowed and pawed at something on the tabletop. Angie returned to the table and spotted a piece of paper with words written on it. "It looks like she left a note for someone." Angie picked up the paper.

"What does it say?" Mee Mee asked.

Angie tilted the paper toward the window's light. "Dearest Carol: Something terrible has happened. There are dark forces at work. I fear I will be blamed for something I did not do. My time here is running out. I am so sad. I have made such a deep connection to our relative who lived in these very woods. Soon the people of Frisco will be at my doorstep, accusing me falsely, just like they accused Cora long ago. I'm not sure what is going to happen to me. Know that I love you. I must . . ." Angie placed the letter on the table next to the cat. "That's all she wrote."

# Chapter 14

Mee Mee stepped toward the open window. "She probably heard us coming as we were talking along the trail." She turned and locked eyes with Angie. "Maybe she heard you say that she was a prime suspect. The wind can carry voices."

"If that's the case," Angie said, "she couldn't have fled too far."

Joel marched toward the door. "Let's split up and see if we can find her."

Angie and Mee Mee followed him outside, and they went off in different directions. Angie checked behind old live oaks and thick pines. She found a deer path and followed it for several hundred yards, constantly glancing to the left and right. *These woods are thicker than a southern accent. She could be hiding in the middle of a thicket right next to me, and I wouldn't see her.* After twenty minutes of searching, she returned to the cabin.

As she cut between some brambles and a yaupon

holly tree, she caught sight of Detective Claudio standing on the stoop and smoking his cigar. Joel approached from the other side, and Mee Mee tromped through the weeds to her right. Joel stopped a few feet from Claudio and brushed some burrs off his beige uniform shirt. Mee Mee caught up with her, and they walked the last few yards to the cabin together.

Claudio removed the cigar, tilted his head and blew out a stream of smoke that snaked upwards and vanished above his black fedora. "Looks like she hightailed it out of here."

Joel let out an exasperated breath. "We've been scouring the woods, but I haven't seen a trace of her."

"Did you ladies have any luck?" Claudio asked.

"No," Angie said.

"Didn't see hide nor hair," Mee Mee grumbled.

Claudio's mouth curved into a smile. "She can't hide forever."

"I know this looks bad," Mee Mee said, "but I can assure you that Cora didn't do anything to hurt that girl."

"I wouldn't be so sure." He thumbed over his shoulder. "I saw all the jars on the shelves in there. Bet some of those plants are toxic. Then there's another shelf overloaded with occult books, witchcraft and the sort."

Angie said, "Did you see the note she left on the table?"

"I read the note. Could be a ploy."

"Wait a minute." Mee Mee took a few steps toward the detective. "Shouldn't a person be considered innocent until proven guilty?"

"In a court of law, maybe. I'm discussing the possibilities here. A pregnant young girl visits a woman who dabbles in the occult. The girl asks her for something to terminate her pregnancy. She takes whatever the woman gives her and then heads back the way she came." He waved the cigar in the direction of the clearing. "After about a hundred yards the poison takes hold, and she stumbles, falls and dies."

"If she stumbled and fell," Angie said, "then why was she lying on her back with her head towards the cabin?"

Claudio shrugged. "She lost consciousness and fell backwards."

"You're jumping to conclusions," Mee Mee said.

"I haven't concluded anything, but the autopsy might. We'll see what the pathologist has to say."

Angie stepped up next to Mee Mee. "Are you going to arrest her?"

"No grounds for an arrest yet." He took a drag on his cigar. "First I want to question her." The gray smoke poured out with every word. "But she's not here, is she? That tells me something."

"She might be out collecting specimens," Mee Mee said.

"Maybe. I know I'm going to collect some specimens off those shelves in there as soon as I get the okay. I'm sure she'll come back here sooner or later. We'll have a talk and see what she has to say." Claudio stepped down from the stoop and nodded at them. "I'd stay and chat a while longer, but duty calls." He shuffled around the cabin but stopped suddenly at the path, turned and faced them. "Deputy Thomas, would you do me a favor? It has to do with this investigation."

"Certainly, Detective Claudio. What do you need?"

"Could you hang out here and keep an eye on the cabin until I hear from Judge Foley. He'll be sending me the warrant digitally. It shouldn't take more than a half hour."

"Sure thing."

"Thank you, sir. And if the woman comes back, tie her to that old live oak behind you so she can't get away." He winked, about-faced and sauntered down the path.

"That poor woman," Mee Mee grumbled. "Claudio is out to get her. I'm surprised he didn't tell you to gather kindling for the witch burning."

"He does seem pretty sure of himself," Joel said.

With the back of her hand, Angie swiped sweat from her forehead. "Cora didn't help her case by fleeing the inquiry."

"True," Joel said. "That's a strike against her."

Mee Mee's upper lip curled. "She felt trapped." She stepped up onto the stoop. "I'll be back in two shakes of a lamb's tail." She entered the cabin.

"What's she up to?" Joel asked. "I'm supposed to

be keeping people out of there."

"Hard to say."

A half minute passed, and Mee Mee exited the cabin. "Okay, now I'm ready to get back to my bookstore."

"What did you do in there?" Angie asked.

"Left my business card on the table. I want Cora to know she can contact me. Are you ready to go?"

"For sure. Let's take the wider trail back to the car. I'm tired of tromping over weeds."

"I'm with you on that."

Angie fluttered her fingers at Joel. "I'll see you at home tonight, hon."

"Love ya, darling." Joel blew her a kiss, walked to the stoop and sat down.

As they headed along the trail, Midnight scampered between them.

"Look who's tagging along," Mee Mee said.

Angie eyed the feline. "I guess no one owns a black cat. They allow you the privilege of their company."

They walked in silence for a couple hundred yards. As they turned onto Pinecone Path, Angie said, "Why are you so convinced of Cora's innocence?"

"Instinct. They say intuition doesn't lie."

"I've found mine to be very accurate, but what if some kind of poison shows up in the autopsy results?"

"Then I won't jump to conclusions like Claudio."

"I'm with you on that. There are other people with motives."

When they neared Old Doctors Road, Angie caught

sight of three youths standing near the path—John Stokes and two of his friends. She recognized the two sidekicks from the incident at the Cora Tree: the acne-faced kid and the boy with the shaved head. As they passed by them, Stokes crossed his arms and raised his chin. The mouths of the other two flattened into hard lines.

Angie glared at them. *What are they doing here? Up to no good, no doubt.* She took a deep breath, shifted her focus to the car and headed down the sandy lane. As they neared the Jeep, she heard Stokes say, "I bet old Cora the Witch poisoned her."

# Chapter 15

Angie managed to back the Gladiator into a patch of nearby weeds and turn the car around. As she drove down Old Doctors Road, the belligerent faces of the three boys invaded her mind and goaded her. She made a right onto Route 12 and said, "Those delinquents are up to something."

"Now you're listening to your instincts."

"Thanks. What are *your* instincts telling you?"

"About those boys?"

"About them and Kiara Bailey."

"Murder."

"You've ruled out suicide?"

The cat had settled onto Mee Mee's lap, and she stroked its head and back. "I think she was a woman scorned, and hell hath no fury like a woman scorned."

"So, orders were issued to terminate her."

"Like you said, she knew too much. A bitter female is more dangerous than a game of Russian Roulette."

"Who did the deed? Stokes?"

"I don't think so."

"Who then?"

"This morning at the top of the lighthouse I heard the short guy tell Stokes not to worry about his girlfriend."

"Good point." Angie rubbed her chin. "Kiara had already been missing for several days. Stokes was getting anxious."

"Right. I'm guessing she threatened to go to the authorities. He told his suppliers, and they murdered her and dropped her body near Cora's cabin. Let the witch take the blame. Thus, the anonymous call."

"They wanted the body to be discovered. Cora has been a horsefly buzzing around their stable. You're thinking like a good detective."

"Maybe I missed my calling."

Angie drove another mile down the road, slowed, turned left and parked in front of the bookstore. "It's been a heartbreaking day. I want to pick up my daughter, give her a big hug, go home and do something ordinary."

"Like dust the furniture?"

"Yes."

"Me, too. I need to check my stock and reorder. The Outer Banks murder mysteries are selling like hot cakes."

"Figures."

A car swung into the space next to the Gladiator. Angie glanced out the driver's side window. *A black Subaru Impreza.* She reached and touched Mee Mee's forearm. "Look who's here."

Mee Mee leaned and peered out the window. "I don't think they're book lovers."

The Impreza's window lowered, and the tall man with the thin mustache twirled his finger.

"He wants me to roll down the window." Angie opened the center console, withdrew the Beretta M9 and rested it on her lap. With her other hand she triggered the window button. The glass lowered.

The Hispanic man gave her a Clint Eastwood squint, turned his head slightly and said, "You ladies should mind your own beesiness. Eet's not healthy to put your nose where eet does not belong."

Angie raised her chin. "It's a free country. We go where we please. I'm guessing you're here illegally."

He wagged his head. "That's no way to welcome tourists. Eet's true. We're visitors. But still, I insist you respect our privacy."

"We haven't done anything wrong. Have you?"

He smiled. "We might." He raised his hand like a pistol.

Angie lifted the handgun and pointed it at him. "Mine has bullets, and it's aimed between your eyes."

His thick brows drew together. "Who are you?"

"Somebody you don't want to mess with. Who are you?"

He smirked. "Have a nice day." The short guy backed the Impreza onto the highway, and they sped south towards Frisco.

"Should we follow them?" Mee Mee asked.

"Are you serious? Remember the last time we tried that?"

"Just offering."

"They'd be watching for us."

"They're trying to scare us into keeping quiet about the drug exchange."

"Now they know we can't be intimidated."

Mee Mee opened her door. "You probably should let your husband know about our little powwow with them."

"I plan on it. Are you going to be okay?"

As Mee Mee stepped out of the car, she pushed Midnight off her lap and onto the seat. "I'll be fine until you see my name in the obituaries." She grinned, shut the door and sauntered to the entrance of the bookstore.

*I don't think she realizes how deep we've dug ourselves into this hole. Hopefully, we won't end up six feet under.* She wiggled her phone out of her jeans pocket and called her husband.

After two rings he answered. "Hey, honeycake, what's up?"

"Are you still at the cabin?"

"Yeah. Haven't heard from Claudio yet."

She informed him about the encounter with the cartel thugs and let him know they headed south toward Frisco.

"That was awful bold of them," he said. "They wanted to know more about you two. Were you harmless tourists or a couple streetwise women who could turn up the heat on them?"

"Now they know."

"I'll alert our dispatcher to give the officers patrolling Frisco and Hatteras a heads up."

"Sounds good." Angie checked her watch. "It's almost time to pick up Phoebe. I'll see you tonight."

"One more thing."

"What's that?"

"About five minutes ago I heard a noise at the side of the cabin. I walked around and saw three young guys standing there. One of them was John Stokes. I asked him what they were doing there. Stokes said they were taking a walk through the woods. Then they left in a hurry."

"We saw them when we were leaving the woods. Obviously, they found out about Kiara's death and the location of her body. I overheard Stokes blame Cora."

"Do you think they were looking for Cora? Maybe they wanted to harm her."

"I don't know, but I'm sure they were up to no good."

# Chapter 16

Cape Hatteras Elementary school was an impressive two-story facility at the end of Middle Ridge Road. Isolated by woods, the sky-blue building welcomed students and parents with its coastal charm. Its decorative gable pediments reflected the traditional design of historic Outer Banks architecture. The school was just the right size, not too big to make a kid feel like a number or too small to lack state of the art resources and technologies. Angie knew most of the teachers and felt confident her daughter was in good hands.

She got lucky and found a parking space not far from where the buses lined up at the front of the school. After getting out of the Jeep, she peered down Middle Ridge Road. *No black Impreza. This is a dead end. That's good and bad. They could easily corner me or be cornered by the cops.* She took a deep breath. *Quit being so paranoid.* She hurried toward the entrance designated for parent pick-ups.

Standing in the shadow of the portico near the front door, a dozen or so parents waited for their kids to be released. A tall woman, wearing a floral print dress, leaned slightly toward a blonde lady and said, "I heard they found the Bailey girl."

"Yes!" the blonde gasped. "My son was a friend of hers. He texted me ten minutes ago. They found her body in the Buxton Woods."

A short bald man wearing black framed glasses stepped up to them. "A friend of mine, an EMT, told me they found her near the cabin where that strange woman lives."

"Cora the Witch?" the tall lady said.

The man nodded. "That's what the kids call her."

The blonde said, "I see her wandering around town all the time with that black cat of hers."

"She's spooky," the tall lady said.

"Do you think she had something to do with it?" the bald guy asked.

"The girl's death?" the blonde said in a hushed tone.

He bobbed his head.

"I'd say she's near the top of the list."

"And it's a short list," the tall woman added.

*Wow.* Angie angled away from them and focused on the school's entrance. *Bad news travels fast in a small town. If it comes down to a trial, I hope those three aren't on the jury. Cora wouldn't stand a chance.* Mrs. Crosby, a brunette middle-aged kindergarten teacher, opened the door and held it open for the kids. A passel of them rushed out and shot off in different directions toward their parents. Phoebe skipped toward Angie, her light blonde high ponytails bouncing with every step.

Angie knelt and spread her arms. Phoebe leapt and hugged her, and Angie lifted and squeezed her tight. "I missed you, Ladybug." A calming comfort flowed over her, something she needed after a day filled with anguish and trepidation.

"I've got something for you in my backpack, Mommy."

Angie lowered her to the ground, and Phoebe slipped out of her backpack, tugged it around her feet and unzipped it. She reached inside and pulled out a piece of yellow construction paper. "It's a picture of our family." She held it up for Angie to see. A stick-figure mother and father held the hands of a small girl between them. The three were brightly colored with red, blue and yellow markers. The girl floated slightly above a rounded stroke of ground with three red flowers dotting the spaces between green grass scribbles. A black cat with pointy ears and a long S-shaped tail stood near the mother.

"Is that Midnight?"

"Yes," Phoebe said. "He's following you."

Angie chuckled. "Yes, he seems to be always following me. Your drawing is beautiful, and so are you. I'll put it on the refrigerator for your dad to see."

"Can you put a title on it?"

"Sure. What would be a good title?"

"A Happy Family."

Angie had to take a quick breath and choke back an emotional surge. Those words struck a poignant chord on a stressful day, but this wasn't a time for tears. Too many people around. She grasped the strap of the backpack with one hand and her daughter's hand with the other. "Come on. I've got a surprise for you in the car."

"Good. I love surprises."

As they passed the bald man with the black-framed glasses, Angie heard him mention Cora again to another guy who had come to pick up his son, a kid from Phoebe's class. The boy asked, "Is she a real witch, Daddy?"

Angie picked up her pace and tugged Phoebe toward the car. *Little kids have big ears. My daughter doesn't need to hear that kind of damning talk.* They beat most of the parents back to their vehicles. Angie opened the back passenger door to put Phoebe into her car seat. While she buckled the seatbelt, the black cat leapt onto the back seat.

"Midnight! Is he my surprise?"

"Yep."

Angie closed the door, got into the car, backed out and headed home.

"See, Mommy. He's always following you. Where's his owner?"

"I don't know. I went to her house today, but she wasn't there."

"Did she disappear?"

"What do you mean?"

"Like a real witch."

"No. She can't disappear or fly on a broomstick."

"Can she turn people into frogs?"

Angie glanced in the rearview mirror to see Phoebe petting the cat. "No. People say a lot of things about her, but don't listen to them. She's just different."

"Midnight is different, too. I wish we could keep him."

"For now, he'll be our guest." She focused on the road and spied a black sedan rounding the turn ahead. She leaned against the steering wheel and blinked to clear her vision. *It's an Impreza.* Her heart thumped like a piston in her chest. As she passed the Impreza she caught sight of a gray-haired lady at the wheel. She took a calming breath and blew it out. *Just a grandmother picking up her grandkid. Man, am I strung tighter than a G-string on a sumo wrestler. Can't wait to get home.*

The five-minute drive home was uneventful. Angie regularly checked her surroundings and the rearview mirror but didn't see the black Impreza or anything unusual. When she turned into her driveway, she noticed a person sitting on the front steps, so she hit her brakes. On second look she recognized Sammy, let off the brakes and parked the Jeep on the right side of the driveway near the steps. The teenager's eyes were red and swollen, and tear lines streaked her face.

Stepping out of the car, Angie asked, "Are you okay?"

Sammy nodded.

Angie opened the back door, and the cat leapt to the ground. Phoebe unbuckled herself and jumped from the Jeep. Midnight pranced over to Sammy, and she gathered the cat onto her lap. Phoebe walked to the steps, sat down next to her and patted Sammy's back.

"I know it's been a terrible day for you," Angie said.

"Kiara was a good friend, and I don't have many good friends."

"I'm your friend," Phoebe said.

Sammy sniffed several times and put her arm around Phoebe. "I know you are."

"Phoebe, please take Midnight in the house and feed him a couple slices of turkey," Angie said. "I need to talk to Sammy alone."

"Okay." Phoebe stood and lifted the cat from Sammy's lap.

Angie mounted the steps and opened the door. "We'll only be a few minutes."

"No problemo, Mommy."

Phoebe entered the house, and Angie shut the door. "She gets that from her father. He's a Schwarzenegger fan."

Sammy tried to smile, but her sniffles quickly erased it.

She sat next to Sammy on the steps. "When did you find out about Kiara?"

"This afternoon during sixth period. Zeke told me and then cut out of class."

"Did he say where he was going?"

"Yeah. He said he had to meet John."

"I saw him, John and another guy in the Buxton Woods. Then my husband caught them standing next to Cora's cabin. I wonder what they were up to?"

"Zeke said that Cora the Witch poisoned Kiara. Maybe they wanted revenge."

"Do you believe Cora killed her?"

"No."

"What do you think happened?"

Sammy wiped her cheeks with her fingers. "I'm not sure. Kiara was upset when she found out that John didn't want her or the baby. She wanted out."

"Out of the gang?"

Sammy nodded.

"What did John say to that?"

"He told her no one leaves his gang. She just walked away from him."

"Who do you think killed her? John?"

"I don't think so."

"Suicide?"

"Maybe an accidental overdose, but I doubt it. I'm not sure what happened, but that woman had no reason to kill her."

"Did you know that John Stokes is a local drug dealer?"

Sammy met Angie's gaze and blinked several times. "Kiara told me she knew some things that could get him into a lot of trouble. So, that's what she meant."

Angie nodded. "His suppliers are very dangerous people. Do you know anything about Mexican drug cartels?"

"Yes. I've seen stories on the news."

"Then you know how they operate. They execute anyone who threatens their business. I saw John Stokes making a dope deal with two cartel members."

Sammy sucked in a quick breath. "Do you think they killed Kiara?"

"We don't know yet. The autopsy results will tell us more."

"I don't want to end up like Kiara." A ding sounded and Sammy funneled her hand into her shorts pocket. "Someone messaged me. It might be my mom." She slid the phone out and checked the screen. "It's from John." She tapped the surface and read the message. "He wants to see me."

"Right now?"

She nodded. "He wants to meet me at Angelo's Pizza."

"What do you think he wants?"

She shrugged. "I'll ask him." She tapped in a message and waited for the reply. He says, 'It's about Kiara. I found out something. I know what happened.'" She responded by saying letters out loud with each touch of her finger: "W-H-A-T-?" She waited, tapping her foot. "Meet me at Angelo's in fifteen minutes, and I'll tell you." Sammy stood.

"Are you going to meet him?"

"I want to find out what he knows."

Angie rose to her feet and locked eyes with her. "He knows Kiara was your best friend. He wants to find out how much you know."

Sammy took a deep breath and swallowed. "I'll be careful. I'll listen to what he has to say and then go on my way."

"Don't go with him anywhere."

"I won't." She walked down the driveway, turned right and disappeared behind a stand of crepe myrtle trees.

# Chapter 17

That evening at about seven o'clock someone knocked on the front door. Phoebe bounded through the family room and into the entry hall. Angie had to double-step to keep up with her. When Phoebe opened the door, Angie immediately recognized the visitor—Sammy's mother. Her sandy blonde hair was slightly darker and shorter than Sammy's, but her dark brown eyes matched her daughter's exactly. She wore a lavender two-piece scrub suit with a V-neck collar.

"Hello, Mrs. Cline. Please come in."

She stepped inside and said, "I'm sorry to bother you, but I'm looking for Sammy. I thought she might be here."

"She was here earlier this afternoon."

"Did she say where she was going?"

"Yes. She got a message from John Stokes. She went to meet him at Angelo's Pizza."

She glanced around the entry hall, the strain in her

eyes intensifying. "When I got home from the clinic an hour ago, I checked my messages. She always let's me know where she's going."

"Did you call her cellphone?"

"Four times. She doesn't answer. I don't trust John Stokes."

"Neither do I."

"With all that's happened lately, I'm really worried about her. I . . . I don't know what to do."

"There're several spots in town where the teens gather. Maybe she's hanging out with friends. I'd be happy to drive you around to those places."

Mrs. Cline smiled weakly. "I'd appreciate that. Hearing about Kiara Bailey's death has knocked me for a loop. She was such a sweet girl. Kids today have to deal with so many issues and temptations. Things have changed since my high school days."

"Amen to that. It's become a world of confusion warped by social media and prowled by predators."

"I've tried to shield Sammy from bad influences, but it's almost impossible."

"Let me get my keys, and we'll be on our way." Angie hurried to the bedroom and snatched her key fob off the dresser. *Joel won't be home for at least another hour. Phoebe will have to come with us. Dear God, I hope we find her.*

They headed out the front door, and Angie made sure it was locked. She led the way to the Jeep, opened the back door and buckled Phoebe into her car seat while Mrs. Cline got into the car. Angie climbed behind the wheel and started the Gladiator. "First stop, Angelo's Pizza."

The restaurant was only a half mile away as the crow flies, but getting there by car required a roundabout route, south on Rocky Rollison Road and then north on Highway 12. Angie figured Sammy had taken the short cut through a few back yards and down Stoney Lane, which came out behind Conner's Supermarket. From there the restaurant was only a five-minute walk.

The pizzeria was a large establishment with white siding and a steep black metal roof. Plenty of parking, a spacious interior and a well-equipped game room offered vacationers and locals a great place to eat and have fun. The teens usually hung out at the picnic tables on the left side of the restaurant. Angie turned right into the parking lot and pulled into a space in front of Angelo's large sign.

"Phoebe and I can walk over to the picnic tables. Would you like to check inside the restaurant?" Angie suggested.

"That's fine with me," Mrs. Cline said. "I'll meet you back here in a few minutes."

As Mrs. Cline headed into the restaurant, Angie helped Phoebe out of the car. They walked across the parking lot toward the left side of the building. Two young families sat at the tables on the front patio. *She's not there. Hopefully, she's at the tables on the left side of the restaurant.* They reached the corner of the structure, and Angie saw three girls, their backs to her, sitting at one of the picnic tables. Holding Phoebe's hand, she hurried to their table to get a closer look, but she could tell by their body shapes that none resembled the statuesque Sammy.

"Excuse me," Angie said.

The girls, two brunettes and a blonde, turned and eyed her.

"I'm looking for a girl named Sammy Cline. Do you know her?"

"Yeah, I know Sammy," the chubby brunette said.

The other two nodded.

"Have you seen her lately?"

"I saw her at school today," the blonde said. Her nose ring and pink lipstick gave her a pop rock panache. "Why do you want her?"

"Her mom is worried about her. She met a friend at Angelo's Pizza this afternoon, but we haven't heard from her since."

The other brunette shifted her leg onto the bench and faced her. She wore a Taylor Swift t-shirt. "Who did she meet at Angelo's?"

"John Stokes."

The three girls made momentary eye contact as if sharing the same thoughts. The blonde tensed her eyebrows and bit her lower lip for a brief moment before she spoke. "She may be over at Fatty's. Sometimes Stokes and his gang hang out there."

Angie gave them a nod and a cautious smile. "Thanks. We'll head over there and see if we can find her." Angie pivoted, took Phoebe's hand and walked toward the Jeep. *They seemed uneasy when I mentioned Stokes's name. They must know his reputation – the local dope dealer.*

"Where are we going now, Mommy?"

"Just up the road a little ways." Angie caught sight of Mrs. Cline coming in their direction. As she approached, Angie asked, "Any luck?"

Mrs. Cline shook her head. "No. I looked around the whole place and questioned the manager. He said he saw a girl matching her description earlier in the afternoon. She left with a tall guy about half past four. Sammy must be with John Stokes somewhere."

"I talked to some girls at the picnic tables. They told me to check at Fatty's. Stokes hangs out there with his crew."

Mrs. Cline peered up the road in the direction of Fatty's. "Okay. Let's keep looking."

After they got into the car, Angie backed away from the sign, shifted into drive and turned right onto Highway 12. She checked her watch: 7:35. *Hope she's there, but I have my doubts. Sammy wanted to find out what Stokes had to say about Kiara. Hanging out with him all day wasn't on the agenda.*

Fatty's, a popular eatery on the north end of Buxton, was only about a quarter mile from Angelo's. After rounding a long turn, Angie made a left into the parking lot of the cedar shingled building. Five cars lined the unmarked spaces along the porch railing in the sandy-gravel lot. Angie maneuvered into a spot facing the steps. A red, white and blue striped flag extended from a porch post with the word OPEN printed on it. Three youths ambled out of the doorway and onto the deck.

"There they are," Angie said. "That's Stokes and his two buddies. Phoebe, you stay in the car and wait for us. This won't take long."

"Do I have to?"

"Yes." Angie met Mrs. Cline's gaze. "Let's stop them before they get to their car."

She and Mrs. Cline exited the Jeep. Stokes and his sidekicks sauntered across the deck. The two women rushed toward the restaurant as the three youths descended the steps toward them.

"Stop right there," Angie ordered.

They halted at the bottom, stiffened and leaned back, their eyes cool but quizzical, appraising them. The acne-faced kid to Stokes's right wore the familiar black Misfits tank top with the grinning white skull. The boy to Stokes's right, the one with a shaved head, stuck an unlit cigarette into the corner of his mouth.

Stokes raked his fingers through his long sandy hair, jutted his thick lower lip, glared at Angie and said, "What do you want?"

"We're looking for Sammy Cline. She was with you this afternoon." Angie's eyes bore into him.

"Who says so?"

Mrs. Cline spoke with hard-edged words. "The manager at Angelo's pizza."

"Who are you?"

"I'm her mother."

Stokes shrugged. "We split a pizza, and then she went on her way. I don't know where she went."

"You demanded that she meet you there," Angie said. "I saw the message you sent her. You said you knew who killed Kiara Bailey."

The skinhead with the cigarette struck a lighter, producing a flickering flame. "Everybody knows who killed Kiara Bailey." He lit the cigarette.

"That's right," Stokes said. "It's no big secret."

"You told her you found something out and that you know what happened," Angie seethed.

"Sure. Cora the Witch poisoned her."

Angie shook her head. "No. You insinuated that you knew more than the false rumors that are floating around. That's why she agreed to meet you. Now where is she?"

"I have no idea."

Mrs. Cline said, "The manager told me you and Sammy left together."

"We went out the door together. She went her way, and I went mine."

"You're lying," Angie fumed. "You know where she is."

"To hell with you. Get out of my way." Stokes cut between the two women, but Angie stuck out her foot and caught his toe. He stumbled and fell onto the ground, his hands skidding on the sand and gravel. He turned onto his rearend and glared up at her. "You dirty bitch! You tripped me."

"It was an accident," Angie scoffed.

"I ought to kick your ass."

"Go ahead and try." Angie put her hands on her hips. "I'd love to see you behind bars for assaulting a defenseless woman."

"You assaulted *me*." He stood and brushed himself off.

The other two edged around the women, keeping their distance.

"I'm a witness," the acne-faced kid said. "You tripped him."

"People with dirty hands always point fingers," Angie said.

He scrunched up his red-dotted face. "What?"

"Let's get out of here . . ." Stokes raised a fist. ". . . before I send that blonde slut to the hospital."

"I'd prefer a battle of wits . . .," Angie sneered, "but you're unarmed."

Stokes spit at her feet, turned and marched toward a red Mustang parked along the deck railing. His two flunkies followed him. They got into the car and slammed the doors. Stokes gunned the engine. As he backed up, he stuck his arm out the window and gave Angie the finger. Then he peeled out in the gravel, kicking up a cloud of swirling dust, and headed south on Route 12.

Mrs. Cline gritted her teeth and raged, "Damn them! They know where my daughter is."

"I believe you're right, but for some reason they don't want us to know. There're a couple more places in Buxton we can check out and maybe a spot or two in Frisco. Do you want to keep looking?"

"Yes. Let's go. You never know. We might find her."

They hurried to the Gladiator. When Angie opened the car door, Phoebe said, "Mommy, why did you trip that guy?"

Angie slid onto the seat, pulled the door shut and started the engine. "I was hoping the fall would knock the jerk out of him, but it didn't work."

Phoebe said, "Mrs. Crosby told us falling down is a part of life. When you fall, just say the ground needed a hug."

Angie couldn't help sneering as she backed out and made a right turn onto the highway. "Yeah, he hugged the ground alright."

She drove through town and stopped at several restaurants, the Orange Blossom Café, Rusty's Seafood and Pop's Raw Bar. No luck. At eight in the evening, nightlife was winding down in the village. Buxton wasn't known for its party atmosphere. People came to the southern Outer Banks to escape craziness. She drove south for another four miles into Frisco to check out the minigolf course and Hank's Ice Cream Shop. They spotted a few teenagers with their families, but obviously, they were tourists.

By the time Angie headed back to Buxton and turned onto Rocky Rollison Road, darkness had descended, transforming the live oaks and tall shrubs along the lane into shadowy creatures. The night breeze enlivened their eerie silhouettes. Angie veered left onto the Cline's gravel driveway and parked near the steps of her prefabricated house.

Mrs. Cline opened the car door. "Thanks for all your help. Please keep Sammy in your prayers."

"We will. Make sure you call the sheriff's office. They probably won't initiate a missing person's case for twenty-four hours, but at least they'll be aware of what's happening."

"I will. Thanks again." She stepped out of the car, closed the door and plodded toward the front deck.

By the time Angie backed out, drove down the road another quarter mile and turned into her own driveway, Phoebe had fallen fast asleep. *Joel's truck is here. Good.* Before exiting the car, she blew the horn in hopes that he would hear and open the front door. She managed to unbuckle her daughter, lift her from the car seat without waking her, turn and kick the door shut.

She mounted the few steps and waited at the door for more than a minute. *Come on, Joel.* After another thirty seconds her patience wore thin, and she fished her keys out of her pocket and managed to open the door while holding Phoebe with one arm. She trudged through the family room and turned down the hallway toward Phoebe's bedroom. When she passed the bathroom, she heard the shower running. *No wonder he didn't hear the horn.*

She entered Phoebe's bedroom, pulled back the Pound Puppy blanket and eased her onto the bed. After removing her sneakers, Angie gently placed the cover over her. *She can sleep in her clothes. Won't be the first time.*

Angie shuffled back to the kitchen, poured herself a bowl of Honey Nut Cherrios and slumped onto one of the yellow-padded chairs. *It's been a long day.* As she savored the sweet bites, scenes from the day replayed in her mind: the morning visit to Cora's cabin, the stakeout at the lighthouse, trailing the cartel thugs, seeing Kiara's body in the Buxton Woods, the confrontation with those same thugs at Mee Mee's bookstore, and the search for Sammy. She felt like she was trapped in a surreal dream.

A few minutes later Joel strolled into the kitchen wearing loose-fitting workout shorts and a white tank top. "Where were you?"

Angie peered up at him, slowly wobbling her head. "Have a seat, and I'll tell you."

Joel pulled out the chair next to her, sat down and planted his forearm on the Formica-topped table. "I'm all ears."

Angie took her time reviewing the details of the day from the time they parted company at Cora's cabin to the search for Sammy.

Joel rubbed his chin, his eyes narrowing. "Those cartel boys are sizing you up. They're trying to determine if you are a threat to their business. That's not good. They don't tolerate interference."

"I know. One girl who interfered is dead, and another is missing. After my clash with Stokes, they might decide to target me."

"It's possible."

"Did Cora ever come back to her cabin?"

"No. Another deputy was assigned to watch the place most of the day, but she never returned. I wonder where she went?"

"Hard to say. She knows that she's the prime suspect."

"What do you think happened to Sammy?"

"I can think of three possibilities. She's hanging out with friends and neglected to let her mom know. Or . . ., I don't even want to mention the other two . . ."

Joel locked eyes with her, his facial muscles tightening. "Abducted or murdered."

# Chapter 18

The next morning Angie dropped Phoebe off at school. The cloudless day did little to brighten her frame of mind. All the way home she tensed up whenever she saw a black sedan. Focused deep breathing didn't help take the edge off her raw nerves or the unsettling lump of lead in the pit of her stomach. As soon as she returned home, she sat down in the kitchen and called Mrs. Cline to get an update on Sammy. Unfortunately, the disheartened mother had no new news to report.

Reading the screen of his phone, Joel entered the kitchen and halted by the table. His face altered into a grim mask. "I just received the results of Kiara Bailey's autopsy."

"Already?"

"Yeah. It doesn't take long for the pathologist to determine the cause of death. The official results won't be released for several weeks."

"Give me the details."

He tilted his head and half-closed one eye. "You might not like hearing this: Kiara Bailey was poisoned."

"Poisoned!" The lump of lead in her stomach grew heavier.

"They found traces of mugwort and hemlock in her system."

Angie planted her elbows on the table and braced her head against her hands. "That's a blow to Cora's claim of innocence." She took several deep breaths, straightened and gazed up at Joel. "I know mugwort can be taken to cause a miscarriage. What's hemlock?"

"Poison hemlock is a highly toxic plant that grows just about everywhere. It has long green stems and sprouts tiny white flowers. You see it along fence lines and in open fields. A small dose can cause paralysis and respiratory failure." He Googled an image of the plant and showed her.

Angie's eyes grew wide. "That's poison hemlock? I've seen it grow along the edges of yards."

Joel nodded. "I've got more bad news."

"What?"

"Investigators found both mugwort and hemlock in the jars at Cora's cabin."

"She swore she didn't poison the girl."

"No one has proven she did. However, the circumstantial evidence is very strong. Kiara visited the woman in hopes of obtaining a natural means of aborting her unborn baby. She died of respiratory failure after ingesting both mugwort and hemlock.

They found her body within one hundred yards of the cabin. It doesn't look good for Cora."

"But someone tipped off the authorities about the body anonymously."

Joel slid his phone into his shorts pocket. "That's true. However, the caller said he was hiking through the woods, spotted the body but didn't want to get entangled in the investigation."

"Or he was lying and was part of a scheme to frame Cora."

Joel stiffened his upper lip. "All the cards are still on the table."

"And I'm not sure which one to turn over." Her cellphone rang, playing James Taylor's *Carolina in My Mind*. She wiggled the phone out of her jeans pocket and checked the ID. "It's Mee Mee." She touched the answer icon and raised the phone to her ear. "What's up?"

"I need you to come over to my guest house next to the store."

"Now?"

"Immediately."

"This sounds serious."

"It is."

"Okay. I'll be there in ten minutes." She ended the call. "That's strange."

"Maybe she heard something about Kiara or Sammy," Joel said.

"Maybe, but she could have told me that over the phone. Something unusual happened. I'll call you and let you know as soon as I find out." Angie stood and kissed her husband, a quick peck on the lips.

"Be careful," Joel cautioned.

"I've got eyes in the back of my head." She turned and rushed through the family room toward the front door.

***

Both Mee Mee's bookstore and guest house were two of the older structures in the village of Buxton. Her connection to customers and business acumen turned her store into one of the most popular stops along the southern Outer Banks. Her purchase of the house next to the store broadened the possibilities of her trade, offering more parking for customers, room to store stock and a place for visiting guests to stay. Angie made a right and parked in front of the guest house. Painted white with a wide veranda, the house reminded Angie of her grandparents' place in Elizabeth City, welcoming and rustic.

She exited the car, trotted up the few steps, crossed the porch and opened the door. "Mee Mee, are you here?"

"Back here!" Mee Mee's voice called from the rear of the house.

Angie hurried through the front room where boxes of books were stored and into the back room which served as a bedroom with an adjoining bathroom. There in the corner, next to Mee Mee on a ladderback wooden chair sat Cora Mangas. She gazed at Angie, dark circles under her eyes. Her wiry black-and-gray-streaked hair hung over her shoulders. The unlit room shaded her long crimson dress the color of dark wine.

"When did you get here?" Angie asked.

"Last night," Cora responded wearily. "I hid in the woods until dark. Then I returned to my cabin and found Mee Mee's card."

"She showed up at my door about ten o'clock," Mee Mee said, "and I brought her here. She stayed the night."

"You do realize you are a prime suspect in Kiara Bailey's murder?"

Cora's grave eyes closed for a few seconds and then slowly opened. "Do they know for sure the girl was murdered?"

Angie nodded. "The autopsy results came back this morning. She was poisoned. The authorities want to question you."

Cora raised her hand and stared at the ceiling. "No one in this town will believe me, but I swear to the Creator of all nature and the Spirit of the Universe I did not poison that girl."

Mee Mee placed her hand on Cora's shoulder. "I believe you."

"I want to believe you, but there's strong circumstantial evidence. The pathologist identified traces of mugwort and poison hemlock in Kiara's system. The investigators found samples of both plants in the jars at your cabin."

Cora's head wagged fiercely. "I did not collect poison hemlock! I have no use for it."

"They found it. How did it get there?"

Cora spread her hands. "I don't know."

"Wait a minute," Mee Mee said. "Maybe those three boys planted it."

Angie sucked in a quick breath. "That's possible. Joel caught them standing by the cabin window. They could have placed a jar on the windowsill or reached in and lowered it to the floor. There may be fingerprints."

"Please," Cora pleaded, "call your husband and tell him about it."

"I will. I'll ask him to find out where the jar with the hemlock was found."

"There's something else Cora wanted to tell you," Mee Mee said.

"What?"

"When I visit the tree, I keep seeing this house in my visions. It's a place where evil is conjured. Its presence casts the shadow of death across this island. Unspeakable things happen there."

*Here we go again with the psychic stuff.* Angie sat on the bed next to her. "We believe there is a house in this area where a Mexican drug cartel has set up its headquarters. Can you describe the house?"

"It's becoming more and more clear every time I visit the tree. I want to go there tonight. I believe the details of the house will come to me."

"What about the investigation?" Angie asked.

"Detectives want to question you."

"Don't turn me in yet," Cora begged. "Give me a chance to connect to the tree's portal."

"I don't know." Sammy's face infiltrated Angie's mind, and she inhaled a slow breath. "There's a teenage girl by the name of Sammy Cline. She was a good friend of Kiara's. Her mother reported her missing yesterday. We think she might have been abducted."

Mee Mee asked, "Do you think she's being held prisoner at the cartel house?"

Angie nodded. "It's possible. Mexican gangs are notorious for human trafficking, and Sammy knows too much about John Stokes and Kiara Bailey."

"Give me a chance to look into the portal of the tree," Cora said. "I promise I'll meet with you and your husband at my cabin at midnight. He can take me to headquarters to be questioned. I have nothing to hide."

Angie glanced at the ceiling and swallowed. *Maybe I should play along. She knew about the drug deal at the lighthouse. Chances are she saw the note. Maybe she discovered something else in the hole of that tree.* "Okay. I'll talk to Joel. He'll let the investigators know that he'll be bringing you in for questioning late tonight. Hopefully, that will appease them."

Mee Mee said, "You're welcome to stay here the rest of the day. I'll drop you off at the Cora Tree whenever you're ready to leave tonight."

"Thank you. I'd like to go to the tree about nine

o'clock. It will be dark. No one will be around. That should give me plenty of time to commune with the ones who see what we cannot see. Then I'll walk to my cabin."

Angie lowered her chin, her focus locking onto Cora's pleading eyes. "Okay, then. We'll meet you at your cabin at midnight."

# Chapter 19

Later that morning Angie went for a ten-mile run. Wearing shades and a Tarheels ballcap, she hoped to alter her appearance enough to keep the cartel goons from recognizing her. She kept her eyes peeled for the Impreza and opted to jog along back roads and side streets in hopes of spotting the black car in front of a house. No luck.

The whole way she kept replaying the conversation she had with Sammy. *Did I tell her too much? What did she say to Stokes?* She eyed the tops of houses, a pink one with white trim, a teal green one, a cobalt blue one with black shutters rising above a thick stand of trees. *They could be holding Sammy captive in any one of these places.* By the time she covered the distance and slowed to a walk at her driveway, it was a few minutes after eleven. *I need to soak in the tub for half an hour and relax.*

Around noon Joel finally heard back from the investigation team. He and Angie had just finished devouring a salad loaded with green peppers, tomatoes, onions and turkey chunks. Angie carried their empty bowls to the sink while Joel concluded the call. He spun his cellphone on the table and said, "Detective Claudio found the jar of hemlock on the windowsill, but there were no identifiable fingerprints, only smudges."

"I knew it." Angie refilled their glasses with iced tea and sat down. "Obviously, it was planted by Stokes and his two lap dogs. I don't remember seeing a jar there when I looked out that window."

"That's not hard proof. We've identified a possible framing attempt. You saw an empty windowsill, and I saw three guys standing by the window. I'll let Claudio know what we witnessed. He'll come to his own conclusions. The big question he'll ask is: Why did they want to frame Cora?"

"Because she was an easy target. Kiara knew too much and threatened to leave the gang. They used a natural means to poison her, plants a wiccan would collect. If Cora could be blamed for the murder, then that would take the heat off them. On the day I saw Cora at the tree, Stokes made it obvious that he didn't want her hanging around. She was a fly in his ointment. If she was communing with her dead relative at the tree, he would have to wait for her to leave before he could retrieve instructions from the cartel."

"So, by framing Cora they take care of two problems."

"That's how I see it."

Joel took a long drink of iced tea. "Do you think they abducted Sammy?"

"Yes." Angie rubbed her forehead. "I hope it wasn't because of something I told her."

"What did you tell her?"

"That Stokes is a drug dealer for a Mexican cartel. I told her we witnessed a deal go down at the lighthouse. Stokes wanted to meet with her to find out how much she knew. If he somehow coerced that information out of her, that would be reason enough to abduct her."

Joel scratched the slight growth of stubble along his jawline. "She's also young and attractive. She'd be an ideal catch for the human trafficking trade."

Angie nodded. "Once they left Angelo's, Stokes probably alerted the cartel thugs, and they followed her home. When she took the shortcut through the woods behind Conner's Supermarket, they went after her."

"Sounds like a good possibility."

"Cora seemed very confident about identifying the cartel house. She begged me to give her a chance to look into that hole in the tree. Who knows? Maybe she'll come up with a clue to help us locate the house."

"I wouldn't count on it. She might be buying time to find a way out of town."

"I hope not." Angie slowly swiveled her head. "I can't figure her out. I'm almost convinced she has some kind of psychic gift. She knew things about us she shouldn't have known. Then there's the drug deal at the lighthouse. She must have seen the message the cartel left for Stokes. Perhaps the message inspired her vision."

"Or she saw the writing on the wall. I just hope she's being honest with us about tonight."

Angie frowned and lowered her head slightly. "Me, too."

Joel scooted his chair from the table and stood. "I've got to get to work. I should be home by nine or nine thirty."

"Good. Marsha will arrive about eleven. We'll head to the cabin around eleven thirty and pick up Mee Mee at her place in Frisco." Angie got to her feet, stepped up to Joel, linked her hands behind his lower back, raised her chin and kissed him, a long tender kiss. His warmth calmed her jangled nerves. She absorbed the comforting feeling, hoping to capture and prolong it for the rest of the day. "I'll see you tonight."

After Joel left, Angie caught up on her private investigation work: background checks, court case research and internet searches on several news reports concerning legal issues. Two hours passed quickly, and she took a break to drink a cup of coffee and snack on a couple homemade chocolate chip cookies.

Thoughts of Sammy invaded her mind, and the sweet morsels did little to ease her fears. *I should have measured my words more carefully when I told her about Stokes. But I warned her about the possibilities. He enticed her into a trap.* She closed her eyes. *Dear God, I pray she's still alive and unharmed. Please protect her from the evil plans of these lowlifes. Give me a chance to find her.* Opening her eyes, she took a sip of coffee. "Amen."

A memory from five years ago emerged from an old pathway of her mind. After investigating a cold case and recent murder, she had tied the deaths to a strange cult that met in one of the old beach houses along Nags Head's Historic Cottage Row. One of the cult leaders, a man by the name of Arnold Crane, came after her, chasing her through the neighborhood. With the build and speed of a linebacker, Crane closed in on her as she sprinted down the street. A car cut between them and plowed into him, bouncing him off the hood and windshield. Angie took advantage of the collision, made a beeline to the nearest house and pounded on the door. A young Sammy Cline opened the door and let her in. Crane somehow struggled to his feet and staggered toward the house. Sammy led her to the attic where they hid while Angie called 911. Crane broke into the house, but officers arrived in time to arrest him at the bottom of the attic steps.

Angie wheeled her office chair back from the computer. *If at all possible, I'm going to return the favor.* Midnight sprang onto her lap, gazed up at her and meowed. *What can you tell me?* She rubbed the top of the cat's head several times. The pendant on its collar caught her eye, and she lifted it with her forefinger to get a better look. *I've seen that symbol before, an A intertwined with an upside-down horseshoe. I don't know, Midnight. What does it mean? I do know that Phoebe loves you and wants to keep you.* She checked her watch: 2:45. *Time to go pick her up.*

After lowering the cat to the floor, she stood and stretched. She picked up her coffee cup, carried it into the kitchen, set it on the sink and headed out the door. The trip to the elementary school was uneventful. She kept her distance from the other parents while she waited for Phoebe to be released. Despite her efforts, she heard rumblings of rumors, scraps of words and names that cast blame and echoed the community's suspicions.

When Mrs. Crosby opened the door, Phoebe bounded out of the building and pranced to her. Angie clutched her hand and hurried to the Jeep. Driving home, she listened to Phoebe's summary of her day: learning new words, painting a picture of Midnight in art class, playing duck-duck-goose in the gym. Just hearing her daughter's voice assured her that life was good, and the struggle against the corruption that unraveled society was worth it. Seeing her house at the end of the driveway reinforced her determination to stay in the fight.

Stepping out of the car, she heard an engine and glanced over her shoulder. A black sedan cruised by. *Was that an Impreza?* She stood on her toes to peer over the crepe myrtle trees. *I can't tell. It might be.* She took several steps to her right, but the car had zoomed out of sight. *It was just a black car. Don't be so paranoid. Geesh!*

She opened the back door, and Phoebe leapt out.

"Come on, Mommy. I want to show Midnight the picture I painted." She scurried to the front steps, toting her backpack, and Angie quickened her pace to keep up. Before going into the house, she glanced over her shoulder again, but the road was quiet.

***

Phoebe was fast asleep by the time Marsha arrived. For the last three years this neighbor proved to be a reliable babysitter, a fun person who loved kids but in no way lax in her efforts to provide safe parameters for a child as rambunctious as Phoebe. Short with shoulder-length auburn hair, her brown eyes flickered with an affability that had quickly won Angie over when they had first met. In her late twenties and unmarried, she often sought Angie's advice about finding the right man. Angie could tell she admired their family and wanted the same stability and happiness for herself.

"Looks like it's going to be a night of watching the *Late Night Show*," Marsha said.

"No wild parties?" Joel queried.

She wagged her head. "It'll be me, a cup of tea, a bag of popcorn and Jimmy Fallon."

Joel chuckled. "If Jimmy Fallon shows up, get his autograph for me."

"Call us immediately if you notice anything unusual," Angie insisted.

"Phoebe and I will be fine. Go do what you need to

do."

"I'll probably be back about one," Angie said. "Joel may have to spend some time at headquarters after he drops me off."

"Then I'll see you about one."

"I'll call if anything changes," Angie assured her.

***

By the time they picked up Mee Mee at her place in Frisco, it was a quarter to midnight. No cars passed them as Joel drove along a back street. On weeknights, all the restaurants and stores closed by eight p.m. Vacationers and locals spent the evenings entertaining themselves at home, playing cards or watching television. Worn out by the day's activities, most people were snoozing by midnight.

Joel, driving his Dodge Ram pickup, turned left onto Highway 12. "Detective Claudio is counting on me bringing Cora in tonight. I hope she's there."

From the back seat Mee Mee said, "Don't worry. She'll be there."

"You've put a lot of trust in her," Joel said.

"I've spent a lot of time with her over the last two days. She's unusual but good at heart. She didn't poison that girl. She came here to explore her ancestry and to make spiritual connections. It's not right to condemn a woman because she doesn't fit in with the rest of us."

"I agree," Joel said, "but I'll let the facts of the case

determine the outcome. Sometimes people aren't what they seem."

"True, but I'm a pretty good judge of character."

Angie said, "Do you think she's psychic?"

"Hmmmm." Mee Mee waited a few seconds before she spoke. "I think we all have a little psychic in us. It's called intuition. Cora just has an extra helping."

Joel turned onto Old Doctors Road, and the overhanging trees and thickets swayed like wary watchmen in the night breeze. The headlights cut a shaft through the darkness, brightening ragged bushes and the dagger-like leaves of dwarf palmettos. The pickup rumbled along the uneven sandy lane, mosquitoes and night bugs swirling in the glow of its headlights. Joel edged off to the side and parked near the Pinecone Path.

As soon as Angie stepped out of the truck, she sniffed something in the air. "Do you smell that?"

Mee Mee took a whiff. "Yeah. Smells like smoke."

"Might be a beach campfire," Joel said.

Angie flicked on her flashlight. "Let's get moving. It's five minutes to midnight." She directed the beam toward the pinecone-scattered path. A slight swath of smoke drifted up through the trees. As they progressed along the trail, the smell grew stronger and the smoke thicker. When they reached the path that led to Cora's cabin, Angie noticed a flicker of flame deep in the woods. She stepped to her left and stood on her toes. "Oh no! Cora's cabin is on fire!"

# Chapter 20

They ran along the narrow path, the rays of their flashlights shifting and skimming over the bushes and tree trunks. As they neared the cabin, Angie saw flames shooting out of the windows and lapping the sides of the logs. Mee Mee charged to the door. When she opened it, a blast of hot air and fire belched out, and she fell backwards onto the ground. Angie helped her to her feet and pulled her away from the heat of the inferno. Fire broke through the roof near the back.

"Cora!" Mee Mee screamed. "Cora!"

Angie gripped her arm to keep her from charging to the cabin. "It's too late, Mee Mee. No one could survive inside there."

"Dear God, I hope she's not in there," Mee Mee gasped.

Joel pulled his phone from his pants pocket and dialed 911. "This is Deputy Joel Thomas. I want to report a fire in the Buxton Woods. It's a house fire, a cabin. Tell them to come down Old Doctors Road. They'll see my truck parked near the path."

The flames shot through the roof and licked the limbs of the overhanging trees as if Satan himself had opened a pit from hell to consume the hovel. Angie stared incredulously at the conflagration. *Who would do this? Stokes and his stooges? Or was it that wood stove and rickety chimney?* Several minutes passed as they watched without speaking, the fire crackling and fizzling. Sirens sounded in the distance.

"I'm going to meet the first responders," Joel said, "I hope they bring plenty of hoses. It's more than a quarter mile between here and the road." He turned and trotted down the path, the beam of his flashlight glancing off the forms of trees.

Mee Mee stepped next to Angie. "Do you think she was in there?"

Angie's head swiveled slightly. "I hope not."

"She came back here to wait for us."

"Maybe someone was waiting for her."

"To murder her?"

Angie nodded.

"Why? They already framed her."

"To keep her from talking. She would have a lot to say in court in her own defense."

"True." Mee Mee let out a deep sigh. "If she's in there, there won't be much left of her."

"Cause of death would be hard to determine. Someone could have strangled her and built a fire in the stove. It wouldn't be hard to make it look accidental."

Mee Mee glanced around the woods. "Or maybe she watched from the shadows."

"That's possible, too. Perhaps some local witch hunter wanted to rid the town of her. What better way than to destroy her home."

"If that's the case, she may be out there somewhere right now in the darkness."

Angie nodded, and the sirens whined louder. "If she's out there, she won't come near with all the pandemonium about to erupt here."

Mee Mee glanced over her shoulder in the direction of the path. "Maybe she headed back to my place."

The roof fell in, and a rush of glowing embers shot up through the limbs.

"Anything's possible, but I wouldn't put stock in it."

A few of the logs from the left side of the structure tumbled into the center, creating a great bonfire. The flames grew hotter, and they backed away.

By the time the firemen ran hoses from the trucks through the woods, the sides had collapsed into a pile of burning timbers. Detective Claudio and two assistants wearing black Polo shirts arrived and watched the raging flames, their faces mutating in the altering light. The firemen turned on the pumps and poured water onto the burning heap for nearly an hour. The woods grew darker as the fire died. The smell of smoke and wet-charred wood irritated Angie's sinuses. She sniffed and itched her nose. Joel and Mee Mee rubbed their eyes and coughed.

Detective Claudio, wearing the same shabby raincoat, strolled in their direction and faced them. "I guess you won't be bringing Cora Mangas in for questioning tonight."

"Looks that way," Joel said.

"Why the delay?"

"What?"

"Why didn't you bring her in earlier?"

"It was on her terms."

"I see. She contacted you and set the rules."

Joel nodded.

"Why didn't you demand she turn herself in immediately?"

Mee Mee stepped forward. "Because he wasn't there."

Claudio raised his eyebrows and appraised her. "I suppose you were."

"Yes."

"Who are you?"

"Mee Mee Roberts."

Claudio furrowed his brow. "Why didn't you drive her to headquarters?"

"She wasn't ready to go."

"You could have put some pressure on her. She's the prime suspect in a murder."

"Do I look like a cop?"

Claudio stiffened his back and frowned. "What do you do?"

"I sell books. Do you read?"

"Not the paperback pulp you peddle, but I do arrest bookstore owners that harbor criminals."

Mee Mee held out her hands. "Go ahead. Put the cuffs on."

Claudio laughed. "I was just joking."

"No kidding," Mee Mee said. "You've got nothing substantial on Cora Mangas. I was doing you a favor by setting up a meeting."

"So, you think she's innocent?"

"I know she is," Mee Mee said.

"Do you have proof?"

"Just my instinct."

"Instinct doesn't cut it."

Angie motioned toward the pile of charred logs. "Innocent or not, if that's her final destination, we may never know."

"That's true." Claudio plugged his stogie back into the corner of his mouth, turned and eyed the smoking rubble. "However, the Cora of legend escaped the witch burning. Maybe this one did, too." He turned and eyeballed Mee Mee. "I'm sure you'll let me know if she did."

Mee Mee's eyes narrowed. "You'll be on the list." Under her breath she said, "at the bottom."

"What's that?" Claudio said.

"I said, 'No problem.'"

Claudio grinned, his cigar angling upwards. "Good. I don't like problems."

As a deputy strung crime tape around the vicinity of the rubble, Angie, Joel and Mee Mee walked back to the Ram pickup. The blackness of the woods brooded over them as their flashlights cut meager swaths through its gloom. The smoke and murky shadows had constricted her chest, and she strained to take in steady breaths. She couldn't shake the feeling that demons had been released from the smoking pit and waited to pounce from behind the gnarled live oaks. *I wouldn't be surprised if flying monkeys show up.* She picked up her pace.

"What do you think, Joel." Mee Mee's voice sounded shivery in the darkness. "Did Cora accidentally set that fire?"

"No way. Someone was out to get her."

Angie said, "They don't want her to be a witness at her own trial."

"That makes sense." Joel turned off the Pinecone Path towards the truck.

"Let's get home," Angie said. "This night feels like a shroud about to smother us."

They entered the pickup, and Joel backed down Old Doctors Road to a spot where he had room to turn around.

As they drove down Route 12 through Frisco, Mee Mee said, "My gut tells me Cora is alive and well."

"We'll know by tomorrow," Joel said. "The CSI team will sort through the ashes for remains."

"It wouldn't surprise me to see her waiting on my doorstep."

Joel made a left down Mee Mee's street, and Angie kept checking both sides of the road in hopes of catching a glimpse of her. When Joel turned into Mee Mee's driveway, the headlights illuminated the front porch.

"I don't see her on your doorstep," Angie said.

Mee Mee opened the door and stepped out of the car. "Well . . ., she may show up later tonight. Stay safe." She closed the door, turned, scurried across the driveway and up the steps.

Joel backed out and headed toward the main road. "Mee Mee's instincts may be on the fritz tonight."

"I agree. Chances are the CSI will find what's left of her under those charred logs."

"It feels like Hell Incorporated has set up shop in our little slice of paradise."

Angie let out a disgusted grunt. "Drugs, overdoses, murder, human trafficking, and now you can add arson to the list."

"Putting our hopes on Cora to help identify the cartel house was a longshot."

"Yeah, but at least we took the shot. I'd rather bet on a hunch than do nothing, even if it's a snowball's chance in hell."

"Right. We'll keep following whatever leads come our way."

Angie's throat tightened. "For Sammy's sake."

Joel bobbed his head. "We'll keep turning over every stone for Sammy."

As they drove down Route 12, Angie looked forward to stepping inside of her house, checking on her daughter and crawling into bed. She wanted this night to go away like a bad dream. When Joel made a left onto Rocky Rollison Road, she checked her watch. "It's almost one thirty. Marsha will be glad to see us." As they approached their driveway, she spotted a dark colored sedan parked off to the side of the road under the boughs of a live oak. *That's odd. I've never seen the neighbor's car parked there before.*

Joel turned into their driveway, and the headlights lit up their front deck. "We're home," Joel said.

Angie leaned forward and clamped her hands on the dashboard. "Joel! Why is the front door half open?"

# Chapter 21

"I don't know." Joel hit the brakes, and the truck skidded to a stop.

"We passed a car along the edge of the road. The neighbors never park there."

Joel opened the console between the seats and pulled out his Colt 45 revolver. "Let's find out."

They flung open their doors, bolted out of the vehicle and rushed toward the porch. The truck's headlights cast their rambling shadows against the house. Joel led the way up the steps, his gun aimed at the door.

As she neared, Angie noticed scuff marks below the knob. "Someone kicked it open."

They entered the foyer. Loud pounding erupted from the hallway that led to the bedrooms.

Joel shouted, "This is the police! Put down your weapons!"

Glass shattered.

They rushed down the hallway and stopped at the

edge of Phoebe's room. "Put down your weapons!" Joel yelled.

A shot blasted a hole through the door. They backed away, and Joel fell to his knees and crawled back to the doorframe.

Angie dropped to the floor and scooted on her elbows and knees beside him. Glass clinked on the floor, and feet scuffled. "They're climbing out the window."

Joel reached up, turned the knob and pushed the door open. Another shot rang out, the bullet piercing the wall opposite the door. Feet thudded on the ground. Joel clawed forward, reached around the doorframe and fired at the window. Feet thudded again, and someone hollered, "Corre!"

They sprang to their feet and charged into the room. Joel angled to the window, leaned out and aimed in the direction of the footsteps. "I can't see them." He raised the handgun and fired skyward twice. A car started in the distance followed by the sound of tires spinning and peeling out on asphalt.

"They're gone," Angie said. "Must have been the two cartel guys who met Stokes at the lighthouse."

Joel pivoted from the window. "Marsha! Phoebe!"

"We're in here," a muffled voice called from the closet.

"The safe place," Angie gasped. "It's okay. Those two men are gone."

A deadbolt slid from its slot, and the closet door opened. Phoebe leapt into her mother's arms and bawled. Marsha, breathing rapidly, stepped out of the closet, closed her eyes and said, "Thank God you showed up."

Joel put his arm around her shoulders. "Settle down. It's all over now. Sit down and take deep breaths." He directed her to Phoebe's bed.

She eased herself onto the mattress and tried to slow her breathing. "I . . . I remembered about the safe place."

"I'm glad you did." Angie glanced at the ceiling and sent up a quick thank you prayer. Several years ago, she felt compelled to turn Phoebe's closet into a safe place. She convinced Joel to replace the flimsy door with a steel door and frame. He added a strong lock that could be engaged from the inside.

Phoebe took a long breath and stifled her sniffling. "I turned the lock like you showed me, Mommy."

Angie squeezed her tighter. "You're a smart girl. I'm so proud of you."

Joel sat on the bed next to Marsha. "Were you asleep when they broke in?"

She wobbled her head. "No. I was flipping through the channels when I heard someone knock. Leaving the chain on, I cracked the door open. There were two men on the porch, a short one and a tall one. Their ballcaps were pulled down, making it hard to see their faces. The short guy said their car broke down, and he wanted to use your telephone."

"Did he have an accent?" Angie asked.

She nodded. "A Mexican accent. I apologized for

not allowing them in and told them to go to the Lighthouse Sports Bar down the road."

"But they didn't listen," Joel said.

"No. Before I could shut the door, the short guy kicked it, but the chain held. I knew we were in trouble. That's when I remembered about the safe place. I ran into Phoebe's room, picked her up and entered the closet. I told her to be quiet. She reached up and turned the lock."

Joel stood and with a sheepish grin said, "I'm glad I didn't put up too much of a fuss about converting that closet."

Angie gave a weak smile. "Common sense, considering our occupations."

"I'm so glad you did," Marsha said. "It took them a while to figure out where we were. When they tried the closet door, Phoebe screamed. That's when they started pounding, but the door held. A couple minutes later you showed up."

Joel walked to the window. "I don't get it. What was their purpose?"

"They came for me," Angie said. "After I picked Phoebe up from school today, I noticed a black car go by. Had to be them. I should have never pulled my gun on them at Mee Mee's store. They know we're onto them."

Joel jiggled his phone from his jeans pocket. "I'll call the sheriff's office and let them know what happened."

Angie lifted Phoebe and set her on the bed next to

Marsha. "I better call Mee Mee. They may be targeting her, too." While Joel called headquarters, Angie took out her cellphone, brought up her contacts and initiated a call to Mee Mee.

After four rings she answered. "Mee Mee here. What's up?"

"It's Angie."

"I know."

"Is everything okay there?"

"Everything is fine. What's happening there?"

"A home invasion."

"Someone broke into your house!"

"Yeah, the two cartel guys. I wanted to give you a heads up in case they came your way."

"If they do, I'll be ready. Is everyone okay?"

"A little shook up but still in one piece. Shots were fired, but no one was hit."

"Were they coming after you?"

"That would be my guess. When they found out I wasn't here, they tried to kidnap Marsha and Phoebe."

"Traffickers plying their trade. Sounds like you got home just in time."

"We did indeed. Do you want Joel to send an officer over to keep you company?"

"Only if he looks like a young Robert Redford. However, I wouldn't mind a beefed-up patrol of my neighborhood. I'll keep Sally Sixshooter on my nightstand. Don't worry about me."

"Okay. Joel will let them know. One more thing."

"What's that?"

"Did Cora show up?"

"Not yet, but I haven't given up hope."

Angie paused for several seconds before she spoke. "Well . . ., we can always hope. I'll talk to you tomorrow."

"Bye."

***

Twenty minutes later someone knocked on the front door. Standing next to Joel, Angie opened it to see Detective Claudio and his two assistants. His shabby, faded raincoat matched the color of his complexion. Angie recoiled at the smell of his cigar smoke that wafted into the house.

"Mind if we come in and talk?" His voice sounded like gravel sliding off a dump truck.

"Not if you get rid of that stogie first."

He plucked the half-consumed cigar from his mouth and tossed it over his shoulder into the driveway. They entered the front hall, and Joel closed the door. Wearing black ball caps with department logos, the two CSI assistants stood behind Claudio and glanced around the room.

"We were waiting for the embers to cool when we heard about the break-in," Claudio said. "Of course, my curiosity got the better of me: Was all this connected or just coincidence? So, here I am."

"What do you think?" Angie asked.

Claudio rubbed the stubble on his jowls. "A young

girl has been murdered. Another one is missing. The prime suspect's cabin has been torched. Whether the suspect is alive or not is yet to be determined. You seem to think she's innocent, and on the night of the fire, your home is invaded. I'm a few pieces short of a full puzzle here. What do you think?"

Angie gritted her teeth. *You're a few pieces short alright.* "The break-in wasn't random."

Joel said, "We believe a drug cartel may be involved."

Claudio straightened. "Whoa! How did you come up with that storyline?"

"The two girls hung out with the same gang of kids," Joel said. "Their leader, John Stokes, is a dealer."

Claudio raised a thick eyebrow. "And Stokes sells dope for a cartel?"

"Yes," Angie said. She recounted their visit with Cora and Cora's vision of the exchange at the tower. Then she told him about the stakeout and confrontation with the two Hispanic men.

"Obviously," Claudio said, "they didn't take kindly to your waving a gun in their faces."

"Not at all."

Joel said, "The Mexican drug cartels are vicious. They eliminate their business problems with bullets. They see my wife and Cora Mangas as a threat."

"But why murder a strange woman who lives in a shack in the woods? Why eliminate the one that you perceive to be their scapegoat?"

"They fear her," Angie said.

Claudio tilted his head slightly. "Because she's a witch?"

Angie shrugged. "They might be superstitious concerning their perception of her lifestyle. Their tattoos reflect occult influence. I know Cora was a bother to John Stokes. Somehow, she knew about him and his criminal activity. She also told us she had a vision of a house where unspeakable things take place."

"The cartel's homebase?"

Angie nodded.

"And you put your chips on the hocus pocus of a gypsy who may also be a murderer?"

Angie frowned. "I don't know what she is. I know a teenage girl may be held prisoner at that house. Like you, I follow leads."

Claudio swiped his hand across his forehead. "I think you're not seeing the rotten egg that's right under your nose." He held up his hand. "But before I give you my perspective on things, I want to talk to your babysitter."

Joel motioned toward the hallway. "She's in the bedroom with my daughter."

"I want to talk to her alone."

"That's fine. You can take her into our bedroom." Joel led Claudio down the hallway.

Angie eyed the two assistants. "I'm going into the kitchen to get a glass of milk. Do you want something to drink?"

The tall one with a baby face shook his head. "We're good."

Angie walked into the kitchen, poured herself a tall glass of milk and sat at the table. She took a long drink and shut her eyes. Blanking her mind, she felt the comfort of the cool liquid coating her throat and stomach. By the time she swallowed the last gulp, the milk had taken the sharp edge off her nerves. *I need a good long sleep. Claudio better not set me off again tonight.*

She headed back out to the front hall. The two deputies stood tapping their feet and checking their cellphones. Footsteps patted down the hallway, and Joel turned the corner followed by Claudio. The detective halted in front of her and placed his hands on his hips.

"Well?" Angie said.

"I'm not convinced the two prowlers were cartel thugs."

"Why not?"

"According to your babysitter, they were Hispanic. Do you know how many Mexicans work on the Outer Banks during tourist season?"

"Thousands. The great majority of them are good people."

He bobbed his head. "But the perps could have been two lowlifes out to burglarize a home."

"What about the disappearance of Sammy Cline?"

"She's a teenager. Maybe she got mad at the world and took off with her boyfriend. She may show up tomorrow."

Angie felt heat rising from her chest into her face. "What about Cora's cabin?"

"That's the rotten egg under your nose. She convinced you to put faith in her . . ." He waved his hand in front of his face as if to clear away fog. ". . . and her hocus pocus visions to buy time. She set fire to her own cabin and took off to avoid prosecution for Kiara Bailey's murder."

The muscles around Angie's eyes and mouth tensed. "I think you're way off. The cartel wanted her eliminated. In the next few hours your CSI team will find her remains in the ashes."

"Maybe." Claudio wiggled a cigar from the breast pocket of his wrinkled shirt. "If you're right, I'll treat your family to a meal at your favorite restaurant. If you're wrong . . ."

"If I'm wrong, I'll buy you a box of decent cigars."

Claudio raised his eyebrows. "Could you make them Cubans?"

"Deal, but if you're wrong something else needs to change."

"What's that?"

"The focus of your investigation."

He wobbled his head and stuck the cigar into the corner of his mouth. "True. I'll reconsider your narrative."

"One more thing."

He raised his chin. "What?"

"Don't light that cigar until you are off my property. It smells like a rotten egg."

# Chapter 22

The next morning Angie sat at the kitchen table and watched raindrops collect, coalesce and dribble down the window above the sink. The gray day added to the despair that weighed upon her spirit. The abomination of Hell's invasion of their island paradise had now breached the sacred confines of their home. *What are we supposed to do? We've committed our lives to upholding the law and opposing evil in this world, but monsters have arrived at our door and kicked it in. We're putting our daughter's life at risk. Do we pick up and leave?*

Footsteps sounded down the hall, and Phoebe entered the kitchen wearing Wonder Woman pajamas and clutching a stuffed unicorn. "Good morning, Mommy."

"Good morning, Ladybug. How are you feeling?"

"I'm okay."

"Do you remember what happened last night?"

"Yes. Marsha carried me into the closet and told me to be quiet. Then someone tried to open the door, and

I screamed. I heard their voices, but I couldn't understand what they were saying. I thought they would get us, but you and Daddy chased them away."

Angie caressed her cheek. "Do you know how much we love you?"

A wide smile broadened her face, and she spread her arms, the unicorn dangling by its tail from her hand. "This much."

"Even more." Angie hugged her and held her close.

"Mommy, isn't it time to get ready for school?"

Angie released her embrace, and Phoebe stepped back. "I want you to stay home with me for the next couple days."

"Really?"

"Yes. After all that's happened, we need some time together. We can read books, play games and watch your favorite shows. Would you like that?"

"That would be fun!"

"Phoebe, how would you like to move away from here and go someplace new?"

She shook her head, her blonde locks swaying. "No. I like it here. I have lots of friends at school, and I love to go to the beach."

"But what about the bad men who came here last night?"

"I'm not worried. You and Daddy are strong, and guess what?"

"What?"

She made a muscle with her free arm. "I'm strong, too."

Angie kissed her forehead. "You are strong."

"Besides, wherever you go, there are bad people."

"How do you know that?"

She tilted her head and pointed into the family room. "I hear about it whenever you and Daddy watch the news."

Angie took a deep breath and blew it out with a low whistle. *The wisdom of a child.* "Come on. Let's get some breakfast. What would you like?"

"Confetti pancakes!"

"Confetti pancakes it is."

***

After breakfast Angie called Mrs. Cline to get an update on Sammy. The downhearted woman didn't have any new information to share. Three days had passed since Sammy disappeared into thin air. Mrs. Cline held it together on the phone, but Angie could tell she was emotionally wrecked. Angie assured her that they would investigate any leads that came up and encouraged her not to give up hope.

The morning passed slowly. She and Phoebe watched *Gabby's Playhouse* and played *Hungry Hippo.* Then Phoebe spent time on her iPad while Angie cleaned up that morning's breakfast dishes. As she put the plates into the dishwasher rack, Joel entered the kitchen wearing his deputy uniform. He held up his cellphone and said, "I just heard from Agent Shepherd from the DEA."

Angie closed the dishwasher and faced him. "What did he find out?"

"Early this morning an FBI agent showed up at the scene of the fire and took over the investigation."

"That's good news. Maybe someone more competent than Detective Claudio will be able to put all the pieces together."

"Agent Shepherd told me that Claudio wasn't too happy about the case being yanked from him."

"Too bad. He'll get over it. I'm sure they'll find another case for him to muddle up. Anyway, I'm glad the FBI is involved. Let them know that I'll be happy to share notes."

"I will." He crossed the kitchen and placed his hand on her shoulder. "That's the good news."

She met his gaze. "What's the bad news?"

"The FBI agent found remains in the ashes, and the pathologist identified them through dental records."

"Cora Mangas?"

He nodded.

Angie trudged to the kitchen table and slumped onto the chair. "I knew it. They wanted to eliminate her and any chance that she could offer information on Kiara's murder and Stokes's drug deals."

"It appears that way."

"And she's the obvious suspect, especially if the fire is determined to be accidental."

"But you and Mee Mee can offer a more informed perspective. If the agent has any sense, he'll take note of all you've discovered."

"I hope he's not another Claudio. A young girl's life is at stake."

Joel glanced down at the black and white tiled floor. "Well . . ., if I hear anything else about the case, I'll give you a call."

"I'd appreciate that." He looked up, and her eyes met his. "Joel, have you ever thought about moving away from here, finding another line of work and starting life anew?"

He shrugged. "I try not to think that far ahead."

"Why not?"

"I want to live in the moment. You've heard the old cliché: Take one day at a time, one step at a time. If we're meant to leave the Outer Banks and start a new life somewhere else, those steps will eventually become evident. In the meantime, I'll take the next step with clear focus."

"But what about last night?"

"What about it?"

"All that happened to us. We put our daughter's life at risk because we're here doing what we do. Don't you ever want to escape?"

"Sometimes I do, but escaping never solves problems. It only leaves them behind."

"What does solve problems?"

Joel smiled. "Taking one step at time, one day at a time with clear focus."

His words filtered through the tangled strands of her anxious thoughts and solidified into a stable base on the shifting sands of their circumstances. *That's what I need to do — focus on today and the next step. Now I just got to figure out what that next step is.*

Her cellphone rang playing *Carolina in My Mind* next to her coffee cup on the kitchen table. She swiped it from the tabletop and checked the ID. "It's Mee Mee." She slid her finger across the answer icon. "What's up?"

"I'm at the store. There's someone here who wants to talk to both of us."

"Who is it?"

"Her name is Agent Carol Toledo. She's with the FBI."

"Okay." *That's a surprise. I assumed the agent was male. It doesn't matter.* "I'll be happy to talk to her. I'm keeping Phoebe at home with me the rest of the week. Do you want to drive her to my place?"

"Sounds good. We'll be there in ten minutes. Bye."

Angie ended the call. *Agent Carol Toledo. Where did I hear that name before? Carol! Now I remember.*

# Chapter 23

Angie's curiosity about the agent's first name heightened her anticipation as she waited for them to arrive. *Probably just a coincidence. There are lots of Carols in this world.* Her memory of seeing the name on the note Cora left at the cabin was crystal clear: *Dearest Carol: Something terrible has happened.* When she first saw the note, she assumed Carol was Cora's relative, perhaps a daughter. She closed her eyes and put a leash on her thoughts. *Don't get carried away. Chances are one in a million.*

Ten minutes passed quickly as she straightened up the house. Carrying a basket of folded clothes into the bedroom, she attempted to organize her observations in preparation for the interview. She set the basket on their unmade bed. *So much to remember.* She exited the bedroom, closed the door and made a quick inspection of the house. Phoebe sat in Joel's recliner in the family room, transfixed on a Blue's Clues game on her iPad. Midnight, curled up on her lap, slept peacefully.

Everything seemed to be in order. A hard knock on the door sounded from the front hall. *They're here.* Phoebe's focus on the iPad remained undisturbed. *iPads and kids. Holy ravioli.*

She hurried into the front hall and opened the door. Standing next to Mee Mee, a woman of medium height and figure, wearing a dark blue blazer with an FBI ID tag, removed her Panama sunglasses and nodded at her. Carrying a black satchel, she resembled a young Cora Mangas. Although her black hair was cut into a wavy bob, her features and build matched Cora's uncannily. Angie had to shake off the odd first impression to ready herself to meet the woman.

"Angie Thomas, this is Agent Carol Toledo," Mee Mee said.

"Hello. Please come in. I'm looking forward to talking with you." Angie stepped to the side, and the two women entered.

"I appreciate your hospitality and your time." Carol Toledo's voice matched Cora's tonal qualities except slightly higher in pitch.

Angie glanced at Mee Mee and noticed how her raised eyebrows and tight lips reflected her own astonishment. *I'm lowering those odds to one in ten.* "Please, let's head to the kitchen. We can talk there."

They followed Angie into the kitchen, and she waved toward the table. "Have a seat. Would anyone like something to drink? Coffee or iced tea?"

"No thank you." Carol Toledo placed her satchel on the table and sat down.

"I'm good," Mee Mee said and took a seat.

Angie sat across from the striking woman and folded her hands on the tabletop. "I'm glad the FBI is looking into this case."

Carol Toledo cleared her throat. "Special Agent Shepherd from the DEA suspects drug activity may be involved in these deaths. Both Kiara Bailey and Cora Mangas may have been targeted by a cartel." She reached for the satchel, lifted it and set it on her lap. "The reason I wanted to talk to you is inside this case."

"What's in it?" Mee Mee asked.

"Your names for one thing."

Mee Mee's and Angie's eyes met for a moment but then refocused on the black case. Carol Toledo unsnapped the top, opened it and gingerly withdrew a singed metal container about the size of a cereal box. She set the container in the middle of the table and lowered the satchel to the floor. "The metal box contains a series of dated letters. Your names were mentioned several times in the writings." She removed the lid and pushed the container across the table to Angie. I've arranged the letters by date. Would you please indulge me and read the letters aloud starting with the top one?"

"Sure," Angie said. "I'm anxious to see what's in them." She picked up the first letter. The heat from the fire had yellowed the page but the writing was legible. At the top Cora had noted the date: *April 12*. "I am enthralled to be in Frisco, the town where Cora perished so long ago. Her blood runs through my veins. I want to know what she knew and feel what she felt. Today I made my first visit to the Cora Tree. As soon as I placed my hands on its bark and stared into the shadow of its depths, I felt her presence. A thousand images passed through my mind: the sea, the face of a child, dunes, woods, a sunset, people dressed in clothes of a bygone era, seagulls and ships. I lost my sense of time. I must have stood there for a half hour or more. When I broke my connection to the tree and stepped back, I noticed a young man standing across the street. He was tall with sandy blond hair. He stared at me as if I had trespassed on his premises. A dread poured over me. A darkness exuded from his soul. I turned and hurried back to my cabin."

Angie placed the letter to the side and met Carol Toledo's gaze. "The young man may have been John Stokes. He was Kiara Bailey's boyfriend."

She bobbed her head slowly. "Read the next one."

Angie read the next five letters which detailed more visits to the Cora Tree and her ethereal connection to her dead relative. In two of the letters, she mentioned how the tall blond youth and his teenage friends gathered around her and harassed her. She vowed to not let them divert her from the path of her spiritual journey. Then she read the letter that mentioned the time Angie intervened and threatened to press charges against Stokes and his crew for hassling her.

She carefully lowered the page onto the pile. "That was the first time I saw her. Some of those kids were vicious in their verbal abuse. I wasn't about to stand by and let them attack her. After the confrontation, I turned around, and she was gone."

The agent's dark eyes, like tinted windows, made it difficult for Angie to know what she was thinking. "Go ahead," she said. "Read the next one."

Angie pinched the corner of the next page with her thumb and forefinger and lifted it from the container. She took a deep breath before reading. "Two visitors came to my door today to return my cat. Their names were Angie Thomas and Mee Mee Roberts. Mee Mee owns the local bookstore in Buxton, and Angie was the woman who defended me yesterday at the Cora Tree. We had a pleasant visit. I did a tea leaf reading for Angie. They warned me that a few of the teenagers may be scheming against me, but I am not afraid. I have powers they cannot fathom. Unfortunately, I have no friends here in Frisco. I hope these two women will become my friends."

"What do you remember about that visit?" Carol Toledo asked.

Mee Mee said, "Cora was an unusual woman and a talented violinist. We could hear the soulful strains of the violin as we walked through the woods. We noticed all the plants she had stored in jars on her shelves and discovered that she was a herbalist."

The FBI rep shifted her eyes to Angie. "What about the tea leaf reading?"

Angie bit her lower lip. *Interesting question. I wonder what she's getting at.* "It was . . . startling. She told me things about my family she couldn't have known."

"Do you think she was psychic?"

"I don't know. I'm not very otherworldly, but her reading impressed me. After Kiara went missing, we visited her about a week later. She told us about a vision she had."

Carol Toledo held up her hand. "Before you say anything else, please read the next letter."

Angie lifted the next page from the box and read. "I am worried. The girl who showed up at my door a few days ago went missing. I refused to give her the plant she wanted that would have caused her to have a miscarriage. Today Mee Mee and Angie visited me to question me about her. I told them the truth. I did not give the girl any mugwort. I hope they believe me. Then I felt compelled to tell them about the recent vision I received when I connected to the tree. For some reason I knew they needed to hear it. Angie seemed to understand. She insisted on leaving after I shared it with them." Angie placed the letter on the table.

"Is that the vision you mentioned before you read the letter?"

Angie nodded.

"Tell me about it."

Mee Mee said, "She had a vision of an exchange that took place on top of a tower. She recognized the tall blond guy in the vision and said that the package contained death."

The agent rubbed her chin. "Do you think she envisioned a drug deal?"

"She did," Mee Mee said. "I witnessed it. We left the cabin and staked out the only tower in town—the Cape Hatteras Lighthouse. I climbed to the top and saw a Hispanic guy hand John Stokes a package."

"That was a risky move for a bookstore owner. Drug suppliers, especially cartels, don't deal kindly with suspected informants. Why did you do it?"

Mee Mee shrugged. "Impulse, I guess. At that point Kiara's body hadn't been found. I thought I might hear something."

"Did you hear anything?"

"Yes. The short guy told John Stokes that his boss would be arriving at the house soon."

The agent templed her hands. "That's an important detail. Did he mention a location?"

Mee Mee shook her head. "Sorry, no."

"So, . . ." She shifted her focus to Angie. ". . . were you impressed with Cora's latest vision?"

"Not really. The unbeliever in me had suspicions. Have you heard about the other missing girl, Sammy Cline?"

"Yes. I was told she hung out with the same group of kids."

"Right. She told me she saw John Stokes retrieve a message from the hole in the tree. She glimpsed the drawing on the note—a tall tower with the number 1245 written on it along with a few words. She couldn't make out the words. My guess is that Cora found that note in a hidden crevasse. Then she realized why John Stokes didn't want her around. She put the note back where she found it."

The agent's dark eyes widened slightly. "Do you believe Cora's claim of a supernatural vision was somewhat deceptive?"

"To a degree. It depends on how you define vision."

"How do you define it?"

"Visions are generated in our minds. Cora saw the drawing, read the words and envisioned the possibility of a drug deal."

"And she wanted you to investigate it?"

"Definitely. She knew that I was a private investigator, and my husband was a deputy. Psychics pick up on subtle details. She could tell John Stokes was trouble by his behavior. When she read my tea leaves, she probably made some good guesses, although I am still amazed at her accuracy."

Carol Toledo shifted in her seat, her left eye twitching slightly. "Why didn't she just come out and tell you she found the message?"

"She hoped to maintain her mystique. Who knows? Perhaps she wanted to be recognized as a crime-solving psychic. That would certainly improve her reputation in town."

The FBI agent pointed at the box. "That brings us to our final letter and another vision. I'm interested to hear your response to this one."

"Okay." Angie lifted the last page from the container and noticed it was dated on the night of the fire. "It is a few minutes past eleven. I have just returned from the Cora Tree. This is the third time I have seen this same dark vision when I stared into the hole. It is a vision of a house where unspeakable things happen. The vision has become clearer every time. The house is blue with black shutters. Its third floor rises above a stand of pines. Death is dealt from this hellhole, and innocent ones are bought and sold here. I plan to reveal what I saw to those who can help put an end to what goes on there." Angie lowered the letter to the table.

"Does this last vision surprise you?"

"Not at all," Mee Mee said. "Cora told us she hoped to help identify the cartel headquarters. I dropped her off at the Cora Tree that night at about nine."

"She begged my husband for another opportunity to connect with the tree before he took her in for questioning. She felt certain she could identify the house. We believe Sammy Cline is being held there."

"Do you think her vision is accurate?"

"It's a lead," Angie said. "Maybe she found another message at the tree. There can't be that many blue houses in Frisco or Hatteras. I ran by one the other day on one of Frisco's back streets. Now that I recall, it was surrounded by pine trees."

"So, you think it's worth investigating?"

"Of course," Mee Mee said. "We need to get on it as soon as possible."

The black cat leapt onto the table, causing Angie and Mee Mee to flinch. The cat took several steps toward Carol Toledo and purred. The FBI agent reached and rubbed its cheeks and asked, "What's the cat's name?"

"Midnight." Angie observed how familiar the connection seemed between the woman and the feline. "There's a missing letter."

Stroking the cat's head, Carol Toledo turned toward Angie. "What letter?"

"On the day Kiara's body was found, Cora left a letter on the table in the cabin. It was addressed to someone named Carol."

"What about it?"

"I assumed Carol was Cora's daughter. Your first name is Carol, and you resemble Cora. Are you Cora Mangas's daughter?"

Her hand slipped away from Midnight and rested on the table. "I . . . I am . . ." Her words halted midsentence, and she swallowed, her full lips tightening into a thin line.

Mee Mee stared at her hand. "You're not Cora's daughter. You are Cora Mangas."

# Chapter 24

Angie flicked her eyes from Mee Mee to Carol Toledo and back to Mee Mee. "That's not possible. I didn't get a chance to tell you yet, but the pathologist identified Cora's remains."

"I don't care." She pointed at the FBI agent. "That *is* Cora Mangas."

"How could it be?" Angie challenged.

Mee Mee extended her arm, her forefinger zeroing in on a small symbol on the back of Carol Toledo's hand. "I recognized the Alpha-Omega tattoo next to the mole."

Angie leaned across the table and stared at the tattoo. "That's the same symbol on Midnight's pendant."

The FBI agent closed her eyes and lowered her head. "Okay, okay. You're both wrong." She raised her head, opened her eyes and gathered the black cat onto her lap. "I am not Cora's daughter. There is no Cora Mangas."

Angie gripped the edge of the table. "You were working undercover?"

She nodded. "For the last five months I've been living in old Doc Garlic's cabin, walking the streets of Frisco and staring into the hole of that tree."

Mee Mee asked, "Did you want the people in the village to think you were mentally unbalanced?"

Angie added, "Or someone obsessed with Cora?"

"Either conclusion would have been satisfactory. Everyone around here knows the legend. I wanted people to become accustomed to my wandering around town and my visits to the tree."

Mee Mee knotted her brow. "Why go undercover as a moonstruck gypsy?"

"Have you ever heard of a man by the name of Joaquin Morales? He's also known as El Guapo or the Handsome One."

"Sounds familiar," Angie said. "Who is he?"

"He is a drug lord climbing the pecking order of the Sinaloa cartel. An informant provided intelligence about his assignment of establishing distribution channels along the east coast. Barrier islands like the Outer Banks bring millions of tourists to these beach communities."

"So, you were sent here to find him?" Angie said.

She nodded. "The first step was to identify a local dealer. That wasn't difficult with the help of Midnight."

"Midnight?" Mee Mee pushed up her tortoiseshell glasses. "The cat?"

"Yes." She scratched the cat's cheek. "Midnight is a highly trained feline."

"I didn't know you could train cats," Mee Mee said. "Cats train you."

A slight smile lifted the corners of Carol's lips. "Believe it or not, it's possible. I've worked successfully with Midnight on several cases." She lifted her hand, showing them the Alpha-Omega tattoo. "That's why I got the tat."

"What is Midnight trained to do?" Angie asked.

"Hang out."

Mee Mee chuckled. "That doesn't sound hard."

"Polydactyl cats have been known to bum food at the local restaurants. When Midnight is assigned an area or person, he will hang out in that area or stick with that person until I send a signal."

Angie pointed to the cat's collar. "I bet the signal comes through the pendant."

"You're right."

"But cats hang out all the time in these neighborhoods," Mee Mee quibbled. "What good does that do?"

"The pendant also serves as a microphone and transmitter."

"Of course," Angie gasped. "Alpha-Omega! All seeing and all knowing. I thought you might be a bona fide psychic. That's how you learned about my family and Sammy's visit!"

Carol narrowed her eyes and bobbed her head. "And that's how I discovered John Stokes was a local dealer. I assigned Midnight to areas where I suspected people may be inquiring about opioids and hallucinogens—restaurant patios and bar parking lots. John Stokes's name came up, and I began to follow him."

"And he led you to the Cora Tree," Mee Mee said.

"People visit the Cora Tree all the time, but I thought it was unusual that a guy his age stopped there regularly. I stayed out of sight, but I could see he was retrieving something from the hole in the tree. That's when I realized the tree was a contact point."

Angie sat up straight. "And that's when you became Cora Mangas?"

Her eyes flashed. "Yes. Becoming Cora would be the perfect guise to access the messages left at the tree. People would think I was batty but attribute my behavior to an obsession with the Cora legend."

"Then you began finding messages left by the dealers," Angie said.

"Correct. I found a slot in the wall of the hole hid by a section of wood. If you didn't know it was there, you would never notice it. I jiggled out the section of wood, found the messages, read them and put them back."

Mee Mee jutted her jaw. "That's how you found out about the exchange at the Cape Hatteras Lighthouse."

"Right, but that's also where you caught on to what I was doing."

Angie pressed her index finger to her cheek.

"Sammy glimpsed the same message — the tower and the number 1245. What did the words say?"

"'Hagamos el trato' or let's make the deal. Once I learned your husband was heading up a drug taskforce, I wanted you to know about it and perhaps gather information. However, I was under strict orders to maintain my cover. That's why the FBI issued the pathology report. They wanted the cartel to believe Cora was dead and no longer a threat to them."

Angie said, "And I assume you want us to keep our mouths shut."

"Exactly."

"What about the last vision, . . . ." Mee Mee blinked several times, ". . . the blue house with the black shutters."

"Before sunrise on the night I stayed at your guest house, I made one more trip to the Cora Tree. In the slot I found a drawing of a log cabin in flames with the numbers 1130 written on it. In Spanish someone wrote the word 'Matar' above the drawing and 'Ven a la casa' below it."

"Kill and Come to the house," Mee Mee interpreted.

She leaned inward. "I knew Stokes would stop by the tree sometime that day to get the note. That evening after you dropped me off, I headed to the cabin and used my wig and some pillows to make it appear that I was asleep. I lit a candle and placed it on a stand near the cot. Then I waited in the woods for Stokes to show up. I knew he would lead me to the cartel house after he set the fire.

"So, you know where the blue house is located?" Angie asked.

She nodded. "He set fire to the cabin and waited by the door to make sure I didn't escape. Then he walked out of the woods and back to Frisco. I followed him to the sound side, and he led me to a house surrounded by pines. A tall fence guarded the house. He entered a code at the gate and was granted access."

"What about Sammy Cline?" Angie demanded. "Do you think they're holding her there?"

"I'm sure of it."

Mee Mee furrowed her brow. "Why doesn't the FBI raid the place?"

"They're dragging their feet. Cartels are well armed. They know a raid could turn into a bloodbath. They also got word that El Guapo may be visiting soon. A raid is in the planning stages, but who knows when they will execute."

"Waiting for them to act may be too late for Sammy," Angie said. "They need to move now."

"I agree. When I came here, I wasn't sure what my recourse would be. The letter addressed to Carol gave me one option of maintaining my cover. I could pretend to be Cora's daughter and still acquire any information you two have gathered. But Mee Mee saw through that. I have considered going rogue, but a solo attempt will be challenging."

"Are you talking about an attempt to rescue Sammy?" Angie asked.

"Yes."

"We could help," Mee Mee said.

"That's asking too much. You would be putting your lives at great risk."

"I've been a risk taker all my life." Mee Mee's face lit up like an Outer Banks sunrise. "When I was younger, I wind sailed on the ocean amidst sharks and six-foot waves. Then I risked everything I owned and started my book business. I've hiked across the Sierra Madres, a land infested with rattlesnakes and scorpions. I'm with you on this."

"Me, too," Angie said.

Carol's eyes met Angie's. "But you have a family, a husband and a young daughter. I think two people will be enough."

Angie swallowed. "I was able to give birth to my daughter because Sammy Cline saved my life six years ago. When she went missing, I vowed to return the favor. None of us are guaranteed tomorrow. All we can do is focus on today and take one step at a time. I'm coming, too."

Carol lowered her eyebrows. "Are you sure about this?"

Angie nodded.

"Okay then. I've got a plan. I've already taken the first step."

# Chapter 25

Carol Toledo rubbed her thumb over the Alpha-Omega tattoo on the back of her hand. "Stokes stops at the Cora Tree every day to check for messages."

Mee Mee said, "So, do you plan to leave Stokes a message?"

"I already did."

"You wanted to keep your options open," Angie said.

"Right. Alone or with help, I wanted the option to move forward. If Sammy Cline is still at that house, we can't delay. Tonight's the night."

Mee Mee leaned against the table. "What did you write on the message?"

"In Spanish I wrote: Encuéntranos en la Casa Rota cerca de la pista de aterrizaje."

Mee Mee tilted her head. "Something about a meeting at a broken house."

Carol nodded. "Midnight picked up one of their drug exchange locations while hanging out at Fatty's.

Stokes told his flunkies that he had to meet someone at the abandoned house near the airstrip. The next day I walked along the beach just north of Frisco near the Billy Mitchel Aerodrome. There's an isolated house there about ready to fall into the ocean. The next good storm may finish it off."

"Why do you want to meet Stokes?" Angie asked.

"I need two pieces of information from him: the code to the front gate and the location of Sammy's confinement. Once we get in, we can't waste time. We need to go directly to where they are keeping her."

Mee Mee screwed up her face. "How will you make him cough up that information?"

"I have my methods." She eyed Angie. "However, your husband could be a big help. Do you think he would be willing to come along?"

"Definitely. He'd insist on it."

"Good. Tell him to bring his gun and handcuffs. Who's the best shot between you two?"

Angie raised her hand. "I achieved the designation of marksman in my handgun class."

"Excellent. Mee Mee, your Jeep Wrangler could easily handle the drive along the beach to the abandoned house."

"I've cruised that beach many a time in that old Wrangler."

"Perfect. You'll be the driver. You and I will pick Angie and her husband up at nine tonight. Make sure you wear a black sweat outfit with a hoodie."

"Sounds good," Mee Mee said, "but what's the

plan?"

"Make Stokes talk and then rescue Sammy. I'll let you know the details once I figure them out. At times we may be flying by the seat of our pants."

Mee Mee grinned. "I've done that before."

***

Wind moaned through the nearby trees as Angie and Joel hurried across the pavement and climbed into the back of Mee Mee's Jeep Wrangler. Earlier that evening they had dropped Phoebe off at Marsha's house. They figured the two cartel thugs were too wary to attempt another home invasion but weren't confident enough in their reasoning to leave Phoebe at home with Marsha. Joel asked an on-duty deputy to cruise by Marsha's place several times an hour just in case a black Impreza showed up.

Mee Mee backed the Jeep out of the driveway. "Figures we'd get a bad weather night. There's a nor'easter about fifty miles offshore coming our way. Like Bob Dylan once sang, 'A hard rain's a gonna fall.'"

Carol said, "Let's hope it holds off until we get Sammy out of there and to a safer place."

"Right," Mee Mee said. "A shelter from the storm." As she drove down Rocky Rollison Road, a few sprinkles dotted the windshield.

Joel said, "At least a hurricane's not coming our way."

Mee Mee turned on her wipers. "Hurricane. That's

another Dylan song. Do you know what that one's about?"

"No," Angie said, "but I'm sure we're about to find out."

"It's a protest song about a black boxer who was unjustly imprisoned. The song inspired a public outcry, and eventually a judge declared a mistrial, and the charges were dropped. Dylan helped set Hurricane Carter free."

"Let's hope we can do the same for Sammy," Carol said.

"Amen to that," Angie agreed.

The intermittent raindrops collected and blurred the road ahead before the swipe of the wiper cleared the glass. Angie's understanding of Carol's plan to extricate Sammy seemed blurrier than the windshield. Obviously, Joel would arrest Stokes when he showed up at the condemned beach house, but how was she going to make him talk? Carol said they might be flying by the seat of their pants, but improvisation and serendipity were poor substitutes for a strategic plan. *I hope she's holding some aces, or we may be in for a white-knuckled night at the poker table.*

At the north end of Frisco Mee Mee turned left onto Billy Mitchell Road. Angie assumed the area would be deserted at this time of night. She was right—no cars in sight. The road curved to the left past a small aerodrome building and the lot where a few planes were parked. They rode along the airstrip for almost a half mile, and then Mee Mee made a sharp right toward the shore.

Carol said, "There's a ramp up ahead where you can access the beach."

Mee Mee raised her hand. "I know it well."

"The house is another half mile down the shoreline. Once we get there, we'll go inside and wait for Stokes."

"I've seen the place many times," Mee Mee said. "Thirty years ago, that house had a fifty-yard clearance. Now high tide pounds its pylons like a heavyweight champion. It's been condemned for over a year."

Carol gazed out her window at the dunes and sea. "And high tide will be here in another two hours."

"And we'll be inside that house? That's not good," Angie said.

"I beg to differ with you."

"What do you mean?"

"High tide can be quite beneficial."

*What is she talking about?* Angie braced her hands on the back of Mee Mee's seat as the Jeep rumbled off the asphalt and onto the sand. The vehicle rocked back and forth over deep dips but gradually leveled out as it turned north onto the wet sand by the shoreline. The headlights caught the crests of breakers that thundered, crashed and rolled up the slope of the bank. She could feel the pull of the slant toward the ocean, her shoulder digging into her husband's arm. *Hopefully, we'll be off the beach long before the waves reach the house.*

A minute passed, and Angie spotted the black hulk of the house against the charcoal sky. Above the ocean, lightning streaked in the distance, but the storm was too far out to sea to hear its thunder. The drizzle had not increased in intensity but still altered the view through the windshield enough to distort the scene into a nightmarish seascape. Angie stifled a wave of fear as the Jeep's headlights lit the skewed steps and deck of the tilted house. *The place is a wreck.*

"Park a good distance beyond the house," Carol instructed. "I don't want Stokes to get a close look at the car."

"He drives a mustang," Angie said. "Hopefully, he's smart enough to park on Interdunal Road and walk over the dunes."

"He's a local." Mee Mee drove past the house. "He knows better. Driving a sports car onto the beach is a tourist's mistake. He'll walk over the dunes." She stopped the Jeep about fifty yards beyond the abandoned house.

The four doors opened, and they exited the Wrangler. A few steps behind, Angie glanced at her partners in this daring escapade. Dressed in black, they walked toward the house like silhouettes against the umber shades of the shore and iron grays of the angry sky. They halted in front of the steps, which slanted to the right halfway up but straightened towards the top. The front deck tilted slightly to the left. They formed a line and climbed the steps cautiously. Bringing up the rear, Angie glanced over her shoulder at the dunes. *No Stokes yet. Hopefully, he'll get here soon.* With every step the wood creaked and shifted perceptively.

Nailed to the front door, a condemned property sign warned them to keep out. Someone had kicked against the knob, breaking the hold of the padlock and deadbolt. Joel grasped the loose knob, shoved and swung the door open. They entered the dark foyer, and Angie, focusing across the room, barely discerned the repetition of stairs rising and fading into the blackness of the second floor.

Carol faced Joel. "Give me your handcuffs."

"Okay." Joel unclasped the cuffs from his belt. "Here you go."

She took the cuffs. "When Stokes gets here, I want Deputy Thomas and Mee Mee facing him. Angie and I will stand behind the door where he can't see us. In the dark, he'll assume you are the cartel reps. Turn your flashlight on him and make sure he sees your gun. Tell him he's under arrest. I'll come up behind him and cuff him."

"Then what?" Angie said.

"Then I'll try to make him talk."

"With these cartel thugs, talking is a death sentence," Joel said. "I'm sure he realizes that."

"There are many ways to die."

As the minutes passed, Angie paced near the base of the stairs. *What is she going to do? Put a gun to his head and threaten to put a bullet through his brain if he doesn't comply? We are in desperation mode here. Without that combination and Sammy's location, we'll be flying blind.* She stopped pacing. *Settle down. Just take the next step.*

Mee Mee walked toward the open door. "I see someone coming," she said in a low voice. "Has to be Stokes."

"Get to your positions," Carol ordered.

Angie double-timed it to the wall behind the door, and Carol Toledo, holding the cuffs, backed toward her. Despite the low whistle of the wind, Angie heard creaking footsteps as Stokes ascended to the porch. The footfalls stopped just outside the door.

"What's this about?" Stokes said.

Angie eyed Joel and Mee Mee standing in the shadows. *Come inside.* She felt her heart thudding. Nobody said a word. The darkness and silence felt like a heavy blanket muting light and sound. *Don't just stand there, you dumb dope dealer. Come inside.*

"Why the meeting?"

Joel cleared his throat and mumbled something.

"What?"

He mumbled again, more like a growl.

"I can't hear you." Stokes entered the house and stepped up to Joel and Mee Mee.

Joel clicked on his flashlight and raised his Colt 45 revolver. "You're under arrest. Don't make any fast moves, or I'll shoot. Put your hands up easy now."

Stokes squinted into the light and slowly raised his hands. "What . . . what's going on?"

Carol stepped from behind the door, snagged his right arm and clamped a cuff onto his right wrist.

"You heard him. You're under arrest." She reached around him, yanked his left arm behind him and cuffed his left wrist.

"Who are you?"

"Deputy Joel Thomas. I'm on the drug taskforce for Dare County."

"What's the charge?"

In a grave tone Joel said, "Arson, attempted murder and accessory to kidnapping."

"You're crazy!"

After Joel stated his Miranda rights, Carol stepped around Stokes and into the light. "Do you recognize me?"

He huffed in a quick breath. "You? How did you . . ."

"How did I what? Escape the fire?"

"You're not her. You're too young."

"I'm back from the dead. Better than ever. You tried to kill me, but I've risen from the flames."

"Who are you?"

"Agent Carol Toledo, FBI. You always called me Cora the Witch. Now I've got some questions for you. After you torched my cabin, I followed you to the cartel house. Where are they keeping Sammy Cline?"

He shrugged. "I have no idea."

Carol drew a semi-automatic pistol from her leg holster and poked the barrel into his chest. "You know."

He frowned and shook his head.

"I saw you enter a code at the gate of the house.

What's the code?"

"I don't remember."

"Listen carefully. You are in big trouble. Do want to spend the rest of your life in prison?"

His face froze into a contemptuous mask.

"We can reduce the charges if you cooperate. Believe me, life is going to get incredibly hard if you don't work with us."

His tense face muscles eased. "You've got nothing on me," he sneered. "You can go to hell."

"Alright. He's not cooperating." She faced Joel. "Deputy Thomas, I'll lead the way down to one of the pilings. I want you to escort him. If he tries to flee, shoot him."

"Will do, Agent Toledo. What pilings?"

She pointed to the floor. "The ones supporting this house."

# Chapter 26

Carol Toledo led the way out the door and down the rickety steps. Grasping the chain of the cuffs with one hand and his Colt 45 in the other, Joel walked a half step behind Stokes. Angie glanced at Mee Mee as they trailed Joel.

"What is she going to do?" Angie whispered.

Mee Mee shrugged. "I don't think she's going below to do a safety inspection."

They descended the steps and Angie noticed that the drizzle had turned into steady sprinkles. When she turned toward the ocean, the wind whipped her hood off. She reached back, snagged the hood, pulled it over her head and tugged on the string to tighten it. She could still make out the crests of the waves. They were starting to slap the front pylons of the house.

Carol shuffled down the slope of sand to the middle of the house and stood next to a thick wooden stilt. Stokes wobbled with every step as he descended to the post but managed to stay upright. Joel helped to steady him. Mee Mee and Angie lagged behind, taking careful steps in the dark.

Stokes eyed the waves and then refocused on the support post. "What're we doing here?"

Carol pulled her handgun from her leg holster and aimed at the middle of Stokes's forehead. "Deputy Thomas, unhook his cuffs and latch him around the post. If he tries anything, I'll blow the top of his head off."

Joel holstered his handgun and handed Angie his flashlight. "Help me out here."

She directed the beam behind Stokes's back to the cuffs. Joel took his key and unlatched the right cuff, grasped Stokes's shoulder and shifted him toward the pylon. "Put your arms around the post."

"Why?" Stokes complained.

Carol planted the barrel of her handgun against the back of his head. "Because I say so."

Stokes hugged the post, and Joel reattached the cuff.

"Now let's try this again," Carol said. "I want to know Sammy's location in that house and the combination to the gate."

"I told you. I have no idea where Sammy is, and I forgot the combination."

A large wave broke against the front pylons, rushed up the slope and soaked their feet.

Carol said, "Is that your decision? You're not going to cooperate."

Stokes glared at her. "That's my decision."

"Okay, then. If that's the way you want it." She motioned toward the Jeep. "Let's get out of here before high tide bashes this house into the ocean." She tromped up the slope along the side of the house.

Mee Mee glanced at Angie, shrugged and followed her. Angie directed the flashlight at Stokes. His eyes grew wide, and his jaw dropped. She turned from him and trailed Joel up the sand bank.

"You just can't leave me here," Stokes whined.

Carol halted and faced him. "We sure can. Don't worry. You'll be choking on salt water in another hour or so. Then it will all be over."

"That's murder!" he yelled.

"Yeah." Carol eyed the waves breaking against the front pylons. "You helped to murder one girl and assisted in the kidnapping of another. We don't care what happens to you. We'll blame it on the cartel boys." She eyed her companions. "Let's get out of here."

Another large wave rumbled, rushed up the slope and doused Stokes's ankles. "Wait!"

Carol turned and faced Stokes.

"I'll talk. I'll tell you the combination."

She eyed Angie, winked and trudged down the slope toward Stokes. "First thing I want to know is where they are keeping Sammy."

"I'm not sure."

She stopped abruptly. "Then we're done here."

"No!" he shouted. Angie directed the light at him. He craned his neck, glimpsed the ocean and turned back to face them. "I'm not sure where they're keeping Sammy, but I do know where they kept Kiara."

"Where?" Carol demanded.

"There's a master bedroom on the top floor. They kept Kiara locked in the walk-in closet."

"And you think Sammy is in that closet, too?"

He bobbed his head frantically. "That's where I'd look first."

"Makes sense." She took several more steps toward him. "Now I want to know the combination to the front gate."

"Okay." He closed his eyes and knotted his brow. "It's 570075."

"Are you sure?"

He opened his eyes and nodded.

Carol shifted her focus to Joel. "Deputy Thomas, stay here with Stokes. We'll call you in the next thirty minutes if the combination works."

"You want to keep him cuffed to the post?" Joel said.

"Of course. If the combination works, you can unhitch him and let the sheriff's office know you need a ride back to headquarters. If it doesn't, leave him there to drown. We'll meet up later."

"Sounds good."

"What!" Stokes croaked. "You're leaving me chained to this post? I told you the combination."

"You heard what I said. If it works, Deputy Thomas will unhook you." Carol pointed to the Jeep. "Come on, ladies. We need to get moving."

She hurried up the slope, and Mee Mee and Angie followed her.

"Wait a minute!" Stokes yelled.

The three women stopped and about-faced. "What now?" Carol said.

"I gave you the wrong combination. The Sinaloa boys will skin me if they find out I squealed."

Carol put her hands on her hips. "That's why I didn't leave you with much of a choice. What's the right combination?"

"750057."

"This one better be right, or you'll be sleeping with hammerheads within the hour."

Stokes hung his head. "It's the right one."

"Good. You don't want to be dead wrong."

# Chapter 27

Trudging through wet sand back to Mee Mee's Wrangler, Angie gazed at the sinister sky. Raindrops splashed on her cheeks, dripped along her jawline and trickled off her chin. Phoebe appeared in her mind clutching her unicorn. Feeling an intense need to embrace her daughter, she crossed her arms against her breasts. *This is getting real. What am I doing here?* She imagined picking Phoebe up and holding her close. *There's too much to risk. I'm willing to attempt a rescue but not haphazardly.* She swiped the rain from her face with her right hand. *Don't panic.* She remembered seeing Sammy for the last time as she walked away to meet with Stokes. *I'm willing to keep going, but I need to know more before I take another step.*

When they got to the car, she climbed into the back seat. Mee Mee opened the driver's door and stepped in. Carol, riding shotgun, took a deep breath, closed the door and said, "That went about as well as expected. Now for phase two."

"Listen," Angie said. "I'm not getting cold feet, but I need to know how we're going to pull this off. How are we going to distract them while we attempt a rescue? You said you had a plan."

"I do." She shifted in her seat and faced Angie.

"What is it?"

"I don't know how many people are at the house. I hope only a handful. Yesterday, I paddled a kayak on the sound side to scope out the back of the property. Outside steps lead up to the third floor. Through the great room window, I saw two men, a short guy and a tall one. There may be more, but I didn't see much activity. There's a gate and a walkway that leads to a dock. I noticed a path through the woods that ended by the walkway. The path leads back to the main highway."

Mee Mee started the engine. "So, we distract them, head up the back steps, rescue Sammy and hightail it out the back gate and through the woods."

Carol raised and lowered her head. "That's the basic plan."

"What if the code doesn't work on the back gate?" Mee Mee asked.

"Usually, you don't need a code to exit a gate." Carol raised her hand like a gun. "But at that point we can blast our way through, if necessary."

Angie creased her forehead. "But how will we distract them?"

Carol raised an eyebrow. "By making a scene at the front of the house."

Angie leaned on her knees. "But that's a huge risk for the scene maker. Are you volunteering?"

Carol wagged her head. "Someone else is."

"Who?" Angie puzzled.

"Cora Mangas." Carol reached into the pouch of her hoodie and extracted a small canister. She aimed its nozzle at the empty back seat and released a jet of smoke. With her other hand she pulled a camera-like object from the pouch, directed it toward the smoke and activated a projection light.

Cora Mangas appeared next to Angie. Her gray-streaked hair and crimson dress wavered on the surface of the smoke. Mee Mee gasped. A voice from the projector spoke with eerie tones: "I am the Spirit of Cora. I have come to seek revenge on those who murdered me." The ghost's face distorted, eyes aflame and mouth a gaping hole. "I curse you who ordered my death. I will drag you to hell. Listen to my words. You are doomed. Your wickedness has turned on you like a demon dog. You will . . ."

Carol turned off the projector. "She carries on for another five minutes."

"That was amazing!" Mee Mee gushed. "Do you work for Jim Phelps and the IMF?"

Carol chuckled. "It's a hologram generator. We have a few high-tech toys at the bureau's research and development department. I can control both the smoke and projector with a remote."

Angie reached and waved her hand through the remaining smoke. "Let's hope those cartel goons get spellbound by Cora's ghost long enough for us to get in and out."

"Many cartel members are intrigued by the occult." Carol said. "I'm counting on superstition and fear to hold their attention, but I offer no guarantees. That's the plan. Are you in or out?"

Angie swallowed and nodded. "I'm in. Let's go."

"Where are we heading?" Mee Mee asked.

"The Frisco Body Shop parking lot."

"Got it." Mee Mee hit the gas and the Jeep lurched forward. She spun the wheel and made a U-turn, the Jeep's tires digging deeply into the sand.

As they headed south along the beach, Angie gazed out her window and caught sight of the abandoned house. She couldn't make out Joel or Stokes standing in the shadows under the crippled structure. She imagined the waves climbing higher up the bank. *By the time we check the gate combination, I bet Stokes will be wet up to his waist. I hope the combination works. Joel won't leave him there to drown. Whether it works or not, he'll uncuff him and take him to headquarters.* She shifted her focus to the windshield. The sprinkles had turned into light rain.

They approached the end of the airstrip, and Mee Mee made a right onto the asphalt ramp that led to Billy Mitchell Road. "That body shop is about a mile north once we get on Route 12."

"Correct. The lane that leads back to the cartel house is across the street from the body shop. The house is isolated, surrounded by tall trees and woods."

"I remember seeing that house on one of my runs," Angie said. "The third floor rises above the trees. The siding is blue with black shutters. I hope Sammy is in that third-floor bedroom closet."

"I'm counting on it. Stokes is still a greenhorn in the criminal syndicate world. I don't think he has the cojones to call my bluff."

"The two cartel thugs aren't rookies," Angie said.

"No. They are assassins. Are you prepared to shoot to kill?"

"Yes, I am."

They rode along the airstrip and passed the aerodrome lot and building. Mee Mee made a right turn onto Route 12 and took a deep breath. "We're really going to do this."

"Yes, we are," Carol said. "Are you scared?"

"Yeah, but I feel alive. Either get busy being born or busy dying."

"Is that another Bob Dylan lyric?" Angie asked.

"More or less."

On the mile ride to the body shop, they only passed two cars. A couple bars in the village offered spots to unwind and socialize, but most vacationers and residents were in for the night by nine o'clock. Mee Mee turned right into the shop's gravel parking lot. The place resembled an airplane hangar, a semi-circular building with an office in front. She looped around and stopped facing the highway.

"How's this for a parking spot?" Mee Mee asked.

"Good." Carol pointed across the road to the right. "That's the lane that leads to the house. I'd guess it's about a hundred yards through the woods to the gate." She shifted in her seat and pointed to the left. "Our escape path exits the woods about fifty yards down the road. We'll run like hell, get in the Jeep and take off."

"When do we call for backup?" Angie said.

"Remember, we're off the grid on this. I'm risking my job to save the girl. Your husband will be hauling Stokes to the jail in Manteo. Once we get back here, give him a call and let him know what's happening."

Angie took a calming breath. "Okay. It is what it is. Let's do this."

The three women exited the Jeep Wrangler, crossed the road and hurried to the narrow lane. Trees overhung the entrance, their thick branches and boughs waving in the strong breeze. The greenery darkened the path ahead but provided cover from the light rain. Walking briskly, Carol led the way. Angie blinked several times to clear her vision, but the murkiness of the surroundings made seeing difficult. *Keep putting one foot in front of the other and watch your step.* Mee Mee walked silently beside her. The only sound was the moaning of the wind through the branches.

A spotlight illuminated the front gate which was fastened to a tall privacy fence. As Angie neared the gate, she noticed a tripwire running along the top of the fence. She didn't see any cameras.

Carol halted abruptly a few feet before the lighted area and held up her hand to signal Angie and Mee Mee to stop. "You two wait here in the shadows. I'll go up to the gate and enter the code. As soon as I get the gate open, I'll head to the front steps to set up the hologram. You two take off to the side of the house. Wait there at the front corner. It will take me less than a minute to set up the smoke screen and projector. Then I'll join you."

"Left side or right?" Mee Mee said.

"The clearer path to the rear is on the left side."

Mee Mee nodded. "Got you."

"Do you remember the code?" Angie asked.

"750057. It's a number palindrome."

"Just checking."

Carol took a deep breath. "Are we ready?"

The two women bobbed their heads.

# Chapter 28

Carol zipped across the lighted entrance to the gate's keypad. She poked in the numbers, the lock released, and the gate swung open. She waved her arm and sprinted toward the front steps. Angie charged from the shadows, through the open gate and across the wide lawn to the side of the house. Mee Mee trailed a few yards behind her.

Angie rounded the corner and pressed her back against the siding. Mee Mee skidded to a stop beside her. Both struggled to quiet their breathing. Leaning beyond the edge of the house, Angie caught sight of Carol kneeling at the base of the steps. *She's setting up the hologram projector.* She drew back. *I need to message Joel.* She slipped her cellphone out of her pants pocket and sent a quick text to her husband: *We're in.*

Mee Mee huffed, "Did you see the two cars parked on the right in the driveway?"

"Yes," Angie answered in a low voice. "A pickup truck and the black Impreza."

"I'm guessing there are three or four people in the house."

Angie nodded. She leaned and watched as Carol rotated while still kneeling and sprung toward them like a sprinter out of the blocks. "Here she comes." Angie nudged Mee Mee with her elbow to make room for Carol, and they edged a few feet beyond the corner.

Carol whipped around the corner and pressed her back to the side of the house. "It's all set." She dug her hand into her hoodie's pouch and withdrew a remote. "Keep calm and believe in ghosts."

Angie heard the front door open. She crouched and tilted her head to get a view of the porch. Footfalls thudded, and the short, bearded guy walked to the top of the steps. He raised a large handgun and panned the yard. "Who ees there?"

The door opened again, and the tall man with the thin mustache plodded across the porch, stood next to the short guy and pointed to the entrance. "The gate ees open. Stokes knows the code. Stokes! Ees that you!"

Carol raised the remote and pressed the button. At the bottom of the steps smoke slowly rose through the raindrops.

The tall one gasped and grabbed the short guy's shoulder. "What ees that?"

Carol pressed another button and Cora's ghostly figure took form on the roiling smoke. The raspy voice from the projector spoke with a mesmerizing timbre:

"I am the Spirit of Cora. I have come to seek revenge on those who murdered me." The ghost's face distorted and reformed, eyes glowing red and mouth a gaping hole. "I curse you who ordered my death. I will drag you to hell. Listen to my words. You are doomed. Your wickedness has turned on you like a demon dog."

The short guy stiffened, his gun wavering as if he didn't know where to aim. "Don't move. I will shoot!"

"You will burn in hell," Cora's ghost raged. "Santa Muerte will not save you."

The door opened again, and someone said, "What's going on?"

"El Guapo!" the tall guy yelped. "It ees the ghost of the witch!"

"Let's go," Carol whispered and took off toward the back of the house.

Angie charged into the darkness, each step like a cat scurrying over unfamiliar terrain. She could hear Mee Mee's feet padding the ground close behind her.

At the back of the house Carol whirled around the corner and headed for the deck stairs. With incredible speed, she shot up the risers that zigzagged from one level to the next. By the time Angie got to the third floor, Carol stood at the sliding glass door working on the lock.

"Got it," Carol said. She deposited some kind of tool back into her hoodie pouch and slid open the door. "Leave it open." They entered the great room, and Carol waved her hand. "Check the doors for the master bedroom."

The open floorplan consisted of a large kitchen and living area with a surround couch and big screen TV. Carol and Mee Mee checked the two doors on the far left, and Angie headed to a door on the right next to the fireplace. As the door swung open, she espied a large bedroom. *This has to be it. Where's the closet?* The first door to the left of the king bed led to a spacious bathroom. She tried the next door. Locked. "Sammy! Are you in there?"

"Yes! I'm here. Who's out there?"

"Angie." She unlocked the deadbolt, but the doorknob wouldn't turn. *It's locked with a key.*

Carol and Mee Mee entered the bedroom.

"She's in the closet," Angie said, "the deadbolt is off, but the knob won't turn."

"Step back," Carol commanded. She raised her knee and kicked the knob with her work boot. After three kicks the knob broke loose.

Angie swung open the door. Sammy stood trembling, eyes wide and mouth agape. Her honey blonde hair had become stringy and face pale.

Angie reached and grabbed her hand. "Are you okay?"

She nodded frantically.

Voices echoed in the stairwell.

"They're inside the house." Carol pivoted toward the door. "Get Sammy out of here and wait for me at the back gate. I'll hold them off."

Angie tugged Sammy out of the closet, through the

bedroom and into the great room. "Hurry." As they tore toward the open sliding door, footsteps echoed in the stairwell, and voices grew louder.

Shots erupted. Angie glanced over her shoulder to see Carol at the top of the stairs, handgun smoking as she aimed at the landing. They dashed onto the deck and scrambled down the steps to the second floor. More shots blasted. *She's got the high ground, but how long can she hold it?* They hurried down the remaining steps. Mee Mee followed a few yards behind. More gunshots rang out. *Carol is going to run out of bullets.*

Angie led the way across the lawn. As they passed the pool, she heard a thud and a loud gasp. She turned to see Sammy on the ground. She had tripped over an unwound hose. Mee Mee came to a stop behind her.

Sammy struggled for her breath. "I feel so weak."

Mee Mee clasped her arms around Sammy's waist and pulled her to her feet. "You can make it. Come on!"

With Angie on one side supporting her arm and Mee Mee on the other, they managed to cross the remaining thirty or so yards to the gate. Mee Mee grasped the handle and pressed the release lever. The gate disengaged from the fence.

"Thank God it opened," Mee Mee said.

Angie held the gate open. "Find the path through the woods and get Sammy back to the Jeep. I'll wait for Carol."

Mee Mee took Sammy's hand and led her through the gate and onto the dock. Angie watched as they scurried along the walkway, stopped about halfway and leapt to the ground. *Good. They found the path.* She faced the house and focused on the third-floor deck. More gunfire. She unsnapped her holster from her gun belt and withdrew her Beretta pistol. Carol bolted though the open door, crossed the deck and flew down the steps.

A few seconds later a man charged onto the deck and stopped at the railing. Carol scurried down the last set of steps. *He's waiting for her to run across the yard.* Angie raised her pistol and fired three times. The man dropped onto his stomach and fired back. Carol zigzagged through the yard. Angie kept firing as Carol sprinted to the gate. Several more flashes of gunfire erupted from the upper deck, but Carol flew through the gate and onto the wooden walkway. Angie fired two more times, turned and sprinted for the dock.

Focusing ahead, she saw Carol run past the point where Mee Mee and Sammy had leapt onto the path. "Carol! The path is back here."

Carol skidded to a stop, about faced and ran towards Angie. "Go! I'll follow you."

Angie sprang from the dock and landed near the path. Her eyes had adjusted to the darkness enough to make out the narrow trail, but she had to slow her pace to discern the twists and turns.

"Hurry," Carol said. "He's coming, and I need to reload."

A shot fired, and the bullet thudded into a tree next

to Angie. Glancing over her shoulder, she saw another flash from the dock. She stopped, whirled and emptied her gun in the direction of the flash.

"Get to the Jeep!" Carol shouted. "I'm reloaded."

Angie turned and scrambled along the path. Gunshots blasted behind her. *Carol is fire! She's fearless.* Ahead she saw where the trail broke through the woods near the highway. As she rushed beyond the cover of the overhanging trees, rain splattered on her face. She turned left onto the highway and dashed toward the body shop. The black shape of the Jeep stood out against the gray of the gravel lot. *Get ready to go Mee Mee.* More shots popped in the distance.

She neared the Jeep and caught sight of Sammy sitting in the back on the driver's side. She circled the car, jerked opened the door and darted onto the back seat. "Turn left! Get going! Watch for Carol. She'll be running toward us." Mee Mee peeled out of the parking lot onto Route 12. Angie twisted and peered through the back window. Headlights brightened the end of the lane that led to the cartel house. She ejected the mag from her Beretta and inserted the spare.

"There's Carol!" Mee Mee said. She drove another twenty yards and slammed on her brakes. Then she leaned over the center consol, grabbed the handle and shoved open the passenger door. Carol leapt in.

Shifting in her seat, Angie focused out the back window. The black Impreza approached the end of the lane, whirled onto the highway and zoomed toward them. "Step on it!" Angie shouted. "They're coming after us."

# Chapter 29

As Carol slammed the door, Mee Mee hit the gas, and the Wrangler roared down the highway.

Angie checked the back window. The Impreza trailed about forty yards behind. A flash lit its side, and a gunshot rang out. "They're firing at us! Sammy, get down." Angie reached and pressed her hand against the teen's shoulder, forcing her head below the window.

"I need to reload again," Carol said.

Angie powered down her window and leaned out. The speed and shimmy of the Jeep made it hard to aim, but she fired three times. She pulled back inside and ducked.

Another shot rang out, and the back window shattered.

"Is everyone okay?" Carol shouted.

"I think so," Mee Mee said. "Hang on. I'm turning back down the airport road and heading for the beach."

"Good idea," Angie said. "That Impreza will get stuck in the sand."

A half minute later Mee Mee hit the brakes and swerved onto Billy Mitchell Road. The Jeep threatened to turn onto its side but recovered and stabilized. They sped past the aerodrome building and parking lot.

To her right Angie could see the airstrip. "Go! Go! Get to the beach!" More shots erupted. "Sammy, are you okay?"

"Yes," she cried.

"Stay down," Angie turned and fired several shots through the back window.

"The road to the ramp is up ahead!" Mee Mee shouted. "Hang in there, everyone!"

The road curved to the right, and Sammy slid across the seat into Angie. Leaning over Sammy, she said, "Try to keep calm." She sat up, shifted and fired another shot out the back window.

Mee Mee made a slight turn onto the road that led to the beach ramp. A few seconds later the Wrangler rumbled across the ramp and onto the sand.

Still peering out the back window, Angie caught sight of the Impreza rounding the turn. "Here they come."

The Jeep bounded over the sand's uneven surface, and Mee Mee veered left toward the shore and abandoned house. As soon as the Impreza drove onto the beach, Carol fired a volley of shots out the front passenger window.

Angie watched as the car plowed forward. "Do

your job, sand." Turning around, she glanced out the windshield. The wipers swished away the downpour. "The rain is soaking the beach. That's to their advantage." The Jeep rumbled down the shoreline for another quarter mile. She turned and focused out the back window. The Impreza had slowed down but kept coming. She raised her handgun and fired twice.

Several flash-bangs erupted from the Impreza. Angie ducked. The Jeep rocked precariously. *They hit a tire.* A large dip in the sand sent the Wrangler reeling onto its left side, jouncing and sliding to a stop. Sammy let out a loud groan. Angie blinked to orient herself. She heard scrambling noises from the front seat. Sammy expelled a loud breath, and Angie realized she was on top of the girl. Her Beretta pistol lay against Sammy's thigh. She snagged the gun and holstered it. Then she reached up, clasped the passenger's side headrest and pulled herself toward the door. "We've got to get out of this car. Sammy, are you hurt?"

"I think I'm okay," she moaned.

"Hurry!" Carol hollered. "Get the door open and get out."

"I can't get this dang seatbelt off," Mee Mee piped.

Angie heard the passenger side front door open and saw Carol's dark form climbing upward. Angie reached for the handle and braced her foot against Mee Mee's head rest. Thrusting forward, she opened the door and managed to get her head outside the Jeep. Beside her, Carol clamored through the opening.

Angie braced her hand on the Jeep's frame and heaved herself upwards. The rain splattered her face, and she heard tires spinning in the sand not far away. *Are they stuck?*

Carol leapt from the car, thudded on the ground and rolled to where a ridge of sand gave her some protection from gunfire. "Jump down and crawl to me," she ordered. "We can take up a defilade here."

Angie managed to raise her knee and plant her foot on the doorframe. With that anchor point she was able to rise and dive forward. Her hands helped to break her fall, and she crawled below the ridge beside Carol.

"There! I got it unbuckled," Mee Mee announced. "I'm coming!"

Angie could make out the dark shape of the Impreza about thirty yards away. She reached and drew her handgun out of her belt holster. The car's wheels spun, but the car didn't move. Then the whir of the spinning stopped, and the passenger door opened. She aimed just above the car door. *Step out of that car, and you're dead.* The driver's door opened.

Mee Mee's head rose from the turned-over Jeep. "I'm here," she whispered.

"They're coming," Carol warned. "Keep cover in the car. We'll handle them."

Mee Mee dropped down.

From the passenger side of the Impreza gunfire erupted, bullets spitting into the sand in front of them. Angie and Carol covered their heads with their arms and backed farther below the ridge. Between shots

Angie heard footsteps charging from the driver's side of the car. The barrage halted, and the footsteps came to stop nearby.

Angie eyed Carol. "Where'd he go?"

"I'm on the other side of your Jeep," A man's voice said. "My gun ees pointed at your friend's head. Toss your weapons out, or I'll splatter her brains across the seat."

Carol's jaw muscles clenched, and she pounded the sand with her fist. "We don't have much choice."

"Do it now, or I'll kill the girl, too."

Angie could hear Sammy whimpering. "Okay. Okay. We'll give up our guns."

Carol flung her pistol toward the black car, and it tumbled across the wet sand. Angie took a deep breath and tossed hers in the same direction.

The voice from the car commanded, "Stand slowly, and put your hands up!"

Angie and Carol got to their feet and raised their hands.

The short man stepped out of the car and shut the door. With his gun trained on them, he walked to where the pistols lay in the sand.

"Okay," the short one said. "You two in the Jeep, climb out and don't do anything stupid. Keep them covered, José."

Angie watched as Mee Mee's head appeared above the door opening. Slowly, she managed to find footholds and rose out of the car. She closed the driver's side door, stood on it, leaned and reached for

Sammy's hand. With Mee Mee's help, Sammy climbed out and crouched on the panel above the tire. Mee Mee shut the back door.

"Can we help them down?" Angie asked.

"No," the short man said. "They can jump."

Mee Mee sat on the edge of the car, shoved off, and landed on her feet. Facing Sammy, she held up her hands, and Sammy repeated Mee Mee's method of descent. Mee Mee broke her fall and held her up.

"Come over here and stand next to your amigas," The short man ordered.

Mee Mee and Sammy trudged through the wet sand, heads lowered. The rain poured on them, and the wind whipped their hair and clothing. The four stood in a line facing the two cartel thugs.

The short one raised his gun and pointed in their direction. "Frisk them. Check for weapons and cellphones." He knelt and picked up the discarded handguns.

One by one the tall guy thoroughly padded them down, took their cellphones and crammed them into his jacket pockets. In Carol's pouch he discovered the remote and used his cellphone flashlight to examine it. "Hey, Diego, what's this? It looks like a garage door opener."

"Maybe eet ees. Let me see."

He walked to his partner and handed him the remote.

The short guy laughed. "Ah ha! This ees the ghost maker." He pointed to Carol. "Shine the light on her face."

José ambled back to the women and directed his cellphone light at Carol. She squinted against its brightness.

"Eet's her," The short one said. "Eet's the witch but much younger. Who are you?"

"Agent Carol Toledo, FBI. If you harm me or any of these women, you will become the prime target of every United States federal intelligence agency."

"Oh no," José, the tall one, sneered. "We're so frightened."

"You should be."

"Yeah," Diego said. "We're shaking in our shoes."

"Like you did when Cora's ghost appeared? You couldn't hold your gun steady."

Diego frowned and glared at her. "But I can now. You are the one who should be frightened."

*Carolina on My Mind* played softly. José patted his hand against his jacket pocket. "Eet's one of their cellphones."

Angie's eyes widened. *That's probably Joel calling me.*

"Toss their phones on the ground in front of me," Diego ordered.

José extracted the phones from his pockets and dropped them into the sand in front of the stocky man. The song kept playing. He lowered his gun to within two feet of the phone and pulled the trigger. With the blast the music stopped. In rapid succession he shot the other phones. He glanced up at the women, grinned and said, "Sorry, your phones just died." He shifted his focus to José. "Call El Guapo and tell him we captured the intruders. Ask him what he wants us to do with them."

José slid his phone from his back pocket and made the call. After a few seconds he said, "El Guapo, we captured all four of them." He nodded. "Yes, the girl, too. What do we do now?" His face darkened. "But our car is stuck in the sand. It needs to be towed." He wobbled his head for what seemed like a half minute. "The third floor? On a night like this?" He grimaced. "Okay. We'll see you there in ten minutes."

"Well?" Diego said.

José inserted his phone into his back pocket. "He said to take them to the third floor of the abandoned house."

"The third floor?"

"Sí. He mentioned hiding places."

Diego laughed. "Right. Places no one will look." He smiled grimly. "For a while, anyway." He waved his gun at the women. "Start walking. The house is four hundred meters that way."

The four females turned and headed north along the shore. As they slogged through the rain, wind and wet sand, Mee Mee said, "What are they going to do with us?"

"What do you think?" Angie muttered.

"Execute us?"

"And then hide our bodies in a third-floor closet or the attic," Angie said.

"Keep your heads, girls," Carol said. "We'll figure

some way out of this."

Sammy, trudging through the sand like a zombie, fell behind. Angie drifted back and clasped her elbow. "Don't give up hope. Joel knows we're out here."

Sammy stopped and met Angie's gaze. "I would rather die than go back with them. They want to sell me like a slave."

"You're not going to be sold or die."

"Get moving!" Diego commanded.

Angie glared over her shoulder at him. "Come on. Let's catch up." She took Sammy's hand and plodded forward.

Several minutes passed as they walked the quarter mile to the house. Approaching the structure, Angie noticed it swayed slightly in the strong breeze. Lightning flashed over the dark ocean, and seconds later distant thunder rumbled. The waves battered the post where Stokes had been handcuffed. *Joel hauled Stokes out of here at least twenty minutes ago. Why'd he call my cellphone? To check on me I suppose. Will he hand Stokes off and come back to look for us?* She shook her head. *He'd have no idea where to find us.* She stared at the third floor as they came to a stop in front of the rickety steps. *We may be on our own.*

"José," Diego hollered. "Use your cellphone's flashlight and lead the way up to the third floor. I'll follow behind."

"I don't like this idea," José complained.

"Shut up and do what I say."

José cautiously ascended the steps, crossed the

porch and entered the house. Mee Mee trailed a few feet behind him followed by Carol and Sammy. Angie could feel the porch wobble as the waves plastered the house's ocean side. She stepped into the house, and the darkness deepened except for the glow of the cellphone's light as it rose on the staircase.

From behind she heard Diego's fiendish voice. "Now we'll see who ees afraid."

# Chapter 30

Blackness engulfed everything below the light. Angie held onto the rail as she ascended, her feet searching for each step. The house's framing creaked, and the wind howled and whistled through cracks in the structure. *This place feels like it's possessed.* José reached the second floor, skirted around the post and mounted the next set of stairs slanting in the opposite direction. The light cast shadow bars from the railings on the walls of the upper stairwell. Behind her, Angie could hear Diego's footsteps. *He'd shoot me in the back if I made a quick move. Be patient. God, please get us out of this deathtrap.*

She made it to the second floor, circled around the post and gazed up to the third floor. José reached the top, turned and directed the light down the steps. He stood to the side, pointed to his right and said, "Stand in the middle of the room. Don't try anything stupid." Mee Mee, Carol and Sammy edged past him and entered the thick darkness of the upper room. As

Angie sidestepped José, she felt the urge to punch him where it hurts but managed to control her rage.

Diego followed her into the room, and José entered last, shining the light around the gloomy space. Angie inspected her surroundings as best she could as the light glanced off the walls. The upper floor appeared to be a spare room, much smaller than the lower floors. A moldy smell penetrated the thick air.

Diego took his phone out of his pants pocket, activated the flashlight app and directed the beam on José and the women. "Keep your gun on them. Shoot to kill if they make any fast moves."

"No problemo." José stuck his hand under the flap of his blue jacket, withdrew a handgun from a shoulder holster and waved it at the women. He winked and said, "Go ahead, make my day. Not bad Clint Eastwood, eh?"

Diego chuckled. "Your Eastwood ees mierda." He turned and walked around the perimeter of the room. At the back, he illuminated two doors.

Swiveling her head, Angie watched him. One door led to a bathroom and the other to a closet. Then he walked to the right corner and aimed the light at the ceiling.

He returned to where they were standing and said, "There ees a closet and an attic access in the corner with one of those pull-down cords.

José grinned. "How convenient."

Carol said, "Imbeciles are often impressed by what is convenient."

José knotted his brow. "What's that you say?"

"Never mind," Carol mumbled. "You wouldn't understand."

"She's trying to make us out to be fools again," Diego said.

"I don't have to," Carol goaded. "I can see you are do-it-yourselfers."

Diego took two steps toward her and slapped her with great force. "Go ahead. Insult me again."

A red hand mark appeared on her cheek as she turned back and glared at him.

José shifted the beam from his cellphone to Mee Mee and Angie. "Two familiar faces—the spies from the lighthouse. Who do you work for?"

"We're both self-employed," Mee Mee said.

"Right. You must want slapped, too." He raised his hand.

"No, sir," Mee Mee protested. "I'm a bookstore owner."

"Of course." Diego stepped sideways, nudged José out of the way and faced Mee Mee. "I remember our little talk at your store. You like books, huh? Better prepare yourself for a sad ending."

"What are you going to do with us?" Angie asked.

Diego winked at José. "What do you think, hermano? Would this blonde bring a good price on the sex market?"

"She's skinny, but she may have skills. What do you do for a living, Blondie?"

"I'm a private detective, and my husband is a

deputy for the Dare County Sheriff's Department. I notified him before you took my phone. They'll be here in a few minutes to arrest you."

"You're lying," Diego said.

"Wait and see."

José frowned, his eyes tensing. "Maybe she ees not."

Diego waved him off. "You *are* a fool to believe her. If her words were true, she never would have told us."

Carol said, "You're both fools if you think you can get away with this."

Diego waved his gun in front of her face. "That's bold talk for a beetch without prospects. You will probably die within the next ten minutes."

"You tried to kill me once, but I'm still here."

"We sent a boy to do a man's job." Diego planted the barrel of his gun on her forehead. "I won't fail."

A large wave crashed against the pillars, and the house shuttered. Diego waved away the gun to catch his balance. José eyed him and said, "El Guapo better hurry."

The sound of an engine cut through the wind's moaning. "Speak of Diablo," Diego chuckled. "He's here."

José took a deep breath. "Good. I want to get out of this house of cards."

The driver cut the engine. No one said anything. The wind moaned, and the waves shook the house again. Despite the din of the storm, Angie could hear footsteps ascending, growing louder. José shifted his cellphone light to the doorway. A broad-shouldered man of average height wearing a black Panama hat entered the room and lowered the beam of his flashlight.

He had a wide face and a thick brown mustache with pointed ends slightly curled. His black short-sleeved Polo shirt exposed well-defined biceps and forearms. He wore stylish black slacks. His crazed grin sent chills up Angie's back.

"Ahhhhh." His eyes narrowed. "The lion finally caught up with the gazelles." He directed his flashlight to the women's faces. "Who are these fleet-footed ladies?"

"The dark-haired one says she ees a federal agent, and the blonde claims to be some kind of detective. The other one is a bookstore owner. You already know our muchacha."

He winked at them. "Nice to meet all of you. My name ees El Guapo."

"Your name is Joaquin Morales," Carol said. "And you're the drug kingpin for the Sinaloa cartel on the East Coast."

He smiled and nodded. "My reputation precedes me. Yes, I wear that crown. And you must be the one who scared the mierda out of my companions."

Carol nodded. "They see dead people. I see stupid people."

"But the ghost didn't fool me." He made a bicep pose with his right arm. "I have more brains in that muscle than they have in their skulls. Would you like to feel eet."

"No thanks," Carol said.

Angie raised her chin. "If you're so smart, then why do you deal dope?"

"My business is simply to supply the demands of the people."

"You're a murderer and a lowlife," Angie said, "Certainly, you realize that we have alerted the authorities. They'll be here any minute."

"She ees lying," Diego said. "We destroyed their phones as soon as we captured them."

"My husband is a local deputy. I called him when we turned onto the beach. I told him we were being pursued by cartel members in the direction of the abandoned house."

"You're bluffing," Morales said. "The law would have been here by now."

"They'll be here any minute," Angie assured him. "If you let us go unharmed, I'll testify on your behalf in court. It could mean a reduced sentence."

"Maybe she ees not bluffing," Morales laughed. "Well, then. If time ees of the essence, we better get moving."

"What do you want us to do with them?" José asked.

"I'll take the girl and bookstore lady with me. Smoke the blonde detective and the federal agent." He glanced around the room. "Find a good place to hide their bodies."

Diego pointed to the right corner of the room. "An

attic access ees over there. I think it has a pull-down ladder."

"Perfect."

"Are we heading back to the house?" José asked.

"No. Things have become too risky. As soon as you dispose of those two, climb into the bed of the truck. My plane is only a mile from here."

"What about tomorrow's delivery?" Diego said.

"I'll cancel tomorrow's delivery when we get to the plane."

José tilted his head. "What if we run into the law along the way?"

Morales pointed to Mee Mee. "That's why I'm taking a hostage with me." He stepped toward Sammy and clamped his hand on her elbow. "This one ees precious cargo."  He eyed Mee Mee. "You. Take my flashlight and lead the way to my truck" He handed her the flashlight. "Remember, my gun will be aimed at your back." He unsnapped the flap on his holster and drew his handgun. "Get going." He gave her a slight shove.

Mee Mee glowered at him but turned, directed the light at the floor and headed out the door toward the stairs.

Morales let go of Sammy. "Follow her."

Sammy hung her head and trailed after Mee Mee.

Diego motioned with his gun towards the wall. "You two, stand over there."

# Chapter 31

Angie and Carol walked grudgingly to the wall. José kept his cellphone light directed at their backs. Angie watched their shadows creep up the wall like grim reapers awaiting their deaths. As they turned to face the two cartel thugs, their eyes met briefly. Angie gulped. "What do we do now?" she whispered.

"Don't panic," Carol replied under her breath.

A wave shook the house, and Angie stepped forward to regain her balance.

Diego glanced at José. "Do you want the honors?"

"I . . . I think you . . ."

Carol pointed at the window. "Morales is going to leave you two behind to take the murder rap."

"Don't listen to her," Diego said. "She's just trying to rattle your cage."

"You'll be in a cage alright," Angie said.

They glared at the women. José protruded his lower lip and said, "Go ahead. You can do the deed."

Diego glanced over his shoulder at the window. "I

say we flip a coin."

"Fair enough. I've got a quarter in my pocket."

Above the thrashing of the storm, they heard an engine start. Carol unfolded her hand toward them. "Before you commit murder, you better make sure El Guapo doesn't take off and leave you in the lurch."

Diego frowned, took a deep breath and blew it out. He walked to the window and peered at the truck parked near the steps. A minute passed, and he said, "He's not leaving us. Let's get this over with." He plodded back to José. "Flip the coin."

José holstered his gun. "Here, hold my phone."

He handed Diego the cellphone and funneled his hand into his pants pocket. Diego stood back and gave him some light. José withdrew the coin, flipped it, caught it and pancaked it onto the back of his left hand.

"Tails," Diego called. When he stepped closer to see the result of the coinflip, a huge wave hit the house. The structure collapsed slightly forward. Both men fell toward them. The girls' backs slammed against the wall. Pushing off the wall, Carol thrust herself forward. Diego stretched out his hands to stop sliding. She kicked him in the head, and he let out a groan. His grip on his gun relaxed. Angie dove on the gun and managed to clasp the handle and trigger. She rolled over to catch sight of José.

The cellphone had landed against the slanted wall. Its light glinted off the squirming form of the tall thug as he fumbled with his holster. He drew his gun.

Angie aimed and fired. The bullet struck his forehead and blew out the back of his skull. He collapsed and slid a few more feet in their direction.

Carol leaned forward to keep her balance. "Give me the gun." Angie handed her the gun and she fired a shot into the ceiling. "El Guapo was expecting two shots."

Angie crawled to the phone that lay against the wall and picked it up. She directed the light to Diego. He wobbled his head, moaned and rose slightly. Carol raised the pistol and whacked his temple. He slumped to the floor.

"That should keep him out for a while," Carol said, "if it didn't kill him."

Angie struggled to get to her feet on the slanted floor. "Let's get out of here! This house is about to tumble into the Atlantic."

"First we need to take their jackets." Carol bent over and tugged on Diego's sleeve. "We'll jump in the back of the pickup. If we put our hoods over our heads, he might not catch on."

"It's worth trying."

Angie helped her remove Diego's blue jacket, and Carol slipped into it. Angie directed the light to José's prone body. Blood had poured from his head and spread on the slanting floor toward the wall. She felt nauseous. *I had to do it. Better him than me.* A shiny object lay next to his hand. "What's that?"

"The coin," Carol said. "It's heads."

Angie grimaced as she eyed the crater in the back

of his skull. "Heads, you lose."

Together they removed José's blue jacket. Angie noticed the unusual weight of the nylon garment. "Our guns are still in the pockets."

"Good. We'll need them."

Angie fished the guns out of the pockets, handed Carol hers and holstered the Beretta. She funneled one arm into the sleeve, and Carol held the other sleeve out to make it easier to insert her other arm.

"Are you ready to fly by the seat of your pants?" Carol asked.

"Do I have a choice?"

"Not really."

"Then let's go."

Carol took the cellphone from Angie and led the way down the disjointed steps. To Angie the decent felt like navigating the skewed passageway of a demented funhouse. With every crash of a wave the structure shook more violently. Angie held onto the railing and leaned one way and then the other to maintain her balance from one floor to the next. Finally, they reached the bottom of the stairs. Looking out the open door, Angie could see that the house had detached from the front deck. The Ford 150 pickup was parked about thirty feet from the deck.

Carol closed the flashlight app and slipped the phone into the jacket pocket. "How's your long-jumping skills?"

"Not good. I was a distance runner in high school."

Carol edged to the door. "It's only about five feet.

You can make it. Pull your hood up." Carol backed up several steps, charged forward and leapt. She landed and managed to stay upright.

Angie pulled her hood over her head and tightened the drawstring. "Here goes nothing." She backed up a couple steps farther than Carol. Clenching her fists, she took off and sprung from the base of the doorframe. Her front foot caught on the edge of the deck, and she lunged forward. Carol snagged her arm to keep her from landing on her face and helped her to her feet. "Thanks," she said in a low voice. "That would have been a bloody nose."

They hurried to the back of the truck and used the bumper to climb into the bed. Lightning flashed a mile or so out to sea, and a second later thunder boomed. The rain poured down. Carol stepped to the front of the bed and pounded on the roof. Angie hunkered down and braced her back against the wall of the bed on the driver's side. As soon as Carol sat across from her, the wheels turned and the truck lurched forward, made a U-turn and headed south along the beach toward the aerodrome.

In a low voice Angie said, "What do we do now?"

"Simple," Carol said. "Shoot him as soon as he steps out of the truck."

Angie nodded. "Good plan. I'll let you have the honors."

"No problemo."

In less than a half minute they passed Mee Mee's overturned Jeep Wrangler and the black Impreza.

Angie shook her head. *I almost died there. Joel and Phoebe would have been on their own.* Her hands shook slightly. She took a deep breath and steeled her nerves. *But I'm still here. Morales isn't taking any chances. He wants to fly out of here fast. He knows the feds are on to him.* She glanced at the truck's rear window and saw Mee Mee's head and shoulders. *Sammy must be up front with him.* As the truck rumbled over the sand, Mee Mee's head bobbed. *Morales could be a valuable resource for the DEA. I wonder if . . .* Angie leaned forward, and in a low voice said, "Maybe we should try to take him alive. Remember, the short guy, Diego, mentioned a delivery."

"That would be ideal, but your friends' lives are at stake."

Morales veered the truck to the right toward the ramp near the end of the airstrip. As the vehicle rumbled over the ramp, Angie braced her back against the wall of the bed again. *Good point. Limit the risk. One shot ends it quickly. Too bad. Joel and Special Agent Shepherd would love to grill him for information.*

Morales drove the truck onto the beach access lane and made a left onto Billy Mitchell Road. Occasional flashes of lightning offered Angie glimpses of the airstrip to her left. *We're less than a half mile away.* She reached into the right jacket pocket and pulled out her Beretta.

Carol eyed her pistol "I'm glad we recovered our guns. I'd rather shoot him with my Glock than the cheap Jimenez the short guy carried. Besides, it's empty. I shot the last bullet into the ceiling."

"Joel says your gun is like your lover."

"Yeah," Carol nodded. "It's all about knowing how to pull the trigger."

Morales turned left into the aerodrome parking lot. Two small planes were parked in the front row next to the building, an old-fashioned bi-plane and a double-propeller model. When Morales turned toward the back of the lot, Angie spotted the only other plane about seventy-five yards away. The white plane's wing stretched across the roof of the cockpit. It had a single nose propeller and three-wheel landing gear. To Angie, the small plane looked like it could hold four or five people. *I think that's a Cessna.* She had researched small aircraft for a client during an insurance fraud investigation.

Morales pulled to within forty feet of the plane and stopped, the truck's headlights illuminating the aircraft like a spotlight. Carol stood and stepped toward the driver's side of the cab. She held her Glock with both hands at belt level, ready to raise and shoot. Angie held her breath, waiting for the door to open. Instead, she heard the driver's side window lowering two or three inches.

"Here are the keys," Morales said. With his thumb and forefinger, he extended a keyring with two keys through the small gap between the window and doorframe. "I need to make two quick phone calls. The girl stays with me. Take the bookstore lady, get into the plane and start the engine."

Carol's eyes tensed as she met Angie's gaze. She lowered the gun, reached across the roof of the truck and took the keys. Angie stood and whispered, "What do we do now?"

# Chapter 32

"I can't get a good angle to shoot him through the window," Carol whispered." She took a step back from the cab and focused on the rear window. "Mee Mee is on the passenger side of the back seat. Climb over and let her out. Keep your back to Morales so he can't see your face."

"Then what?"

"While you're letting Mee Mee out, I'll hustle to the plane, unlock the door and climb in. That way he won't see us together and compare heights. Once you and Mee Mee get into the plane, I'll get in position to shoot him when he steps out of the truck."

Angie let out an uneasy sigh. "I hope this works."

"We're flying by the seat of our pants." Carol hopped off the back of the truck and hurried to the plane.

Angie climbed over the side and knocked on the back passenger window. The lock released. She opened the door, keeping her back to Morales. When

Mee Mee stepped out of the truck and caught sight of Angie's face, she huffed in a sharp breath.

"What's the problem?" Morales barked.

Mee Mee shook her head and said, "I'm frightened. Where are you taking me?"

"Shut up! Put her in the plane!" he ordered.

Angie locked her hand onto Mee Mee's arm and turned her toward the plane. She noticed Carol fidgeting with the keys under the wing. "Go slowly until we get to the beam of the headlights. Then cross quickly to the plane."

"Got it. Nice jacket by the way."

"Yeah. Standard cartel issue."

As they skirted the pickup's front bumper and angled toward the plane, Carol managed to insert the right key and open the door. Keeping her head lowered, she stepped into the plane.

"Hurry," Angie whispered. They entered the headlight's beam and scurried across the lot to the shadows under the wing. As Mee Mee climbed into the cockpit, Angie eyed the truck's windshield. *I hope he's making that phone call and not paying attention to us.* Mee Mee crossed to the passenger front seat, and Carol waited in the back seat to give Angie plenty of room to dart into the cockpit. Angie kept her head low, stepped into the plane and sat in the pilot's seat. She turned and faced Carol. "Do you think he suspects anything?"

"Maybe." She clutched the pilot's headrest and leaned forward.

"Can you shoot him from there?" Angie asked.

"Yes. Just enough room. When he steps out of the truck, I'll grip the top of the door, rise up and fire."

A parking lot light behind the pickup silhouetted the two figures in the front of the truck. Morales appeared to be talking on a cellphone. Sammy trembled visibly. He lowered the phone and remained still.

"What's he waiting for?" Mee Mee said.

Angie glanced at the instrument panel. "He gave us orders to start the plane. He's waiting to see if we know how to start it."

Mee Mee leaned and examined the panel. "Give me the keys."

Carol handed her the keys. She inserted a key into the ignition, pulled out the throttle, flipped two knobs and turned the key. The engine roared to life, the propeller whirling.

Angie gaped at her.

Mee Mee shrugged. "I took flying lessons on a Cessna about ten years ago."

Angie shook her head. "That shouldn't surprise me." Another minute passed. "The plane started. What's he waiting for?"

"He suspects something," Carol said.

The driver's side door opened, and the interior light came on. Morales reached and jerked Sammy across the console into his lap. He stepped out of the truck and ducked behind the door. When he rose up, he held Sammy in front of him, keeping his head down.

"He's onto us," Carol fumed. "He's using her as a human shield."

Morales placed his pistol against Sammy's temple and scooted her forward into the headlight's beam. Terror blanched Sammy's face as Morales lifted and dragged her to the side of the plane.

Carol lowered her handgun. "I can't get a clear shot. Too risky."

"Get out of the plane!" Morales yelled. "I want to see your faces."

The three women glanced at each other and shook their heads.

"Now!" he screamed. "I swear I'll blow this girl's brains out! Get out with your hands up."

Angie holstered her Beretta, stepped out of the plane and raised her arms.

"I knew it," Morales sneered. "You are too skinny to be Diego and your friend is too short to be José."

In a low voice Mee Mee said, "You go next."

Carol looked askance at her.

"You heard me. Go."

Carol slid her handgun into her leg holster, edged around the pilot's seat, stepped to the ground and raised her hands. Mee Mee moved to the pilot's seat.

"When the plane started, I had my doubts." Morales gazed up at Mee Mee. "You. Hands up!"

Mee Mee raised her hands. "I'm not armed."

"But your friends are. You stay right there. Two hostages are better than one." He shifted his focus to

Angie and Carol. "You two, drop your guns to the ground in front of me." He pressed the barrel of his gun more forcibly into Sammy's temple. She squeezed her eyes shut and whimpered.

Angie drew her Beretta out of her belt holster and laid it on the ground a few feet from him. Carol removed her Glock from her leg holster and dropped the firearm next to Angie's.

Morales relaxed, lowered the handgun and redirected his aim at the two women. Gripping Sammy by the arm, he tugged her aside and kicked Angie's weapon under the plane. It spun and skidded, stopping below the whirling propeller. He did the same with Carol's, and it landed a foot or so from the Beretta. "Do what I say," he commanded. "Get away from the plane." He pointed to a spot to the right on the asphalt about fifteen feet from where they stood.

Angie and Carol paced slowly to the spot, turned and faced him.

"Adios Senoritas." He slowly raised his gun.

The Cessna's engine roared as the front wheel turned sharply right. The tail of the plane whipped around and whacked Morales's arm and side. He hit the ground, and his gun skittered across the asphalt toward the two women. Sammy tumbled onto the ground to where the plane once sat.

Angie's eyes grew wide as she watched Mee Mee taxi the plane around the parking lot toward the entrance. Morales scrambled on his hands and knees toward his gun. Carol charged forward and kicked the weapon before he could reach it. The gun tumbled and skidded toward the middle of the parking lot.

Morales staggered to his feet and surged toward the gun. Carol leapt and tackled him by the ankles. He turned over, kicking violently. His foot conked Carol on the head, and she slumped over.

As he struggled to stand, Angie slammed into him from the side. He rolled over and sprung to his feet. She tried to attack him from the front, but he whipped her around and put her into a front headlock. Angie, clutching his arm, watched Sammy pick up one of the guns that Morales had kicked under the plane. She whirled around and aimed in their direction. "Let her go!" she screamed. Angie heard the plane's engine grow louder.

Sammy drew closer, raising and pointing the gun at Morales's head. "I said let her go! I swear I'll shoot!"

Morales released the headlock and shoved Angie into her. Sammy fell backwards and dropped the pistol. Angie landed on top of her. Morales turned and dashed toward his gun. The parking lot light illuminated the plane as it headed back in their direction.

Angie scoured the ground for the pistol as the roar of the plane's engine neared. *There it is.* She turned onto her stomach and reached for the pistol. Morales picked up his gun and whipped around to face her. The plane closed in on him. He turned to avoid a collision, but the propeller sliced off his right arm and flung it into the air. Angie watched as the appendage cartwheeled over her head. His gun landed between her and Sammy. She looked up and saw that Mee Mee had stopped the plane. Morales lay on the ground, squirming and screaming.

# Chapter 33

Mee Mee cut the engine.

Angie glanced at Carol. She rubbed the bump on her forehead and struggled to her hands and knees. Angie and Sammy rushed to her side and lifted her to her feet.

"Help me!" Morales wailed.

Supporting Carol, Angie on one arm and Sammy the other, they plodded to where Morales lay. As they neared to within a few feet, they saw him clutching the stump of his shoulder and writhing in pain. Blood dripped between his fingers.

"I'm dying," he sobbed.

Mee Mee dipped under the wing and halted inches from the crimson pool that puddled around his shoulder. Her eyes grew wide. "I didn't mean to kill him."

Carol blinked several times and shook her head. "Don't worry. You only winged him."

"Do something," Morales groaned. "I'll bleed out.

Call for an e-squad."

"Why should we?" Carol sneered.

"I know things." His eyes flamed with fear. "I don't want to die and burn in hell."

Angie let go of Carol's arm and leaned on her knees. "The man named Diego mentioned a big delivery."

"Yes. Cocaine and fentanyl. Stop this bleeding, and I'll give you the details."

Carol scoffed, "You're not in any position to negotiate terms."

"What?"

"You heard me. I want to know when, where and who. Right now. Then I'll stop the bleeding."

"Okay, but I want legal immunity, too."

"No way. Tell me now or you'll die like a dog in the next five minutes."

"I'll tell you." He took several gasping breaths. "The delivery is tomorrow at the house you raided. They'll arrive after dark."

"Tell me who is coming?" Carol insisted.

"El Mayo and his men."

"Raphael Perez?"

He nodded. "He's coming to deliver the drugs and talk about big moves."

Carol eyed Angie and said, "He's a major boss in the Sinaloa cartel."

"I saw him talking on his cellphone," Angie said. "He probably cancelled the delivery."

"I swear I did not. I called someone else." He took

in several painful breaths. "Ask the girl."

Carol focused on Sammy. "Is he telling the truth?"

Sammy bobbed her head. "He called someone by the name of Fernando and asked him to pick up his truck."

"I'm telling you the truth," he whined.

Carol took off her jacket. "Santa Muerte is with you tonight, but hell still awaits your arrival." She knelt next to him, covered his shoulder with the jacket and applied pressure.

He grimaced in pain. "Someone call 911. Please!"

"We would," Angie said, "but your boys destroyed our phones."

"Use mine," he pleaded. "It's in my pants pocket."

Angie dropped to her knees and wiggled the phone from his front pocket. "What's the code?"

"Eleven-one-two. Hurry. Everything . . . is getting . . . foggy."

Angie entered the numbers.

"Before you call 911, check his recent calls."

Angie tapped on the icon. "Only one call in the last two hours. That would have been the call to Fernando."

"Good. Make the 911 call and then contact your husband. Tell him we've got some information the DEA will be anxious to hear."

Mee Mee asked, "What about the two guys back at the abandoned house?"

"Geesh!" Angie said as she dialed the number. "I almost forgot about them."

Carol cringed. "Better tell them to send an e-squad and cruiser down there, too. Let them know there may be a live one."

Mee Mee leaned on her knees. "What happened down there?"

Carol's eyes met hers. "We had a tag team match, but it wasn't a fair fight."

"But they had guns."

"Yeah, but we had the ocean."

Angie held the phone to her ear. An operator answered and said, "911, what's your emergency?"

"We have two locations where we need emergency crews and officers."

"To whom am I speaking?"

"This is Detective Angie Stallone. I'm using someone else's phone. My husband is Deputy Joel Thomas."

"Go on."

"The first location is at the Billy Mitchell Aerodrome parking lot. A man by the name Joaquin Morales had his arm severed by a propeller. Please inform the officers that Morales is a drug lord for the Sinaloa cartel."

The voice on the other end of the line hesitated for several seconds. "Okay. What's the other location?"

"A mile north of the airport along the beach is an abandoned house. Two of Morales's men are on the top floor. One is dead, and the other is unconscious, at least he was fifteen minutes ago. We disarmed him, but he still may be dangerous."

"Anything else, Detective Stallone?"

"Yeah, the house is about ready to fall into the Atlantic Ocean if it hasn't already. We'll be waiting at the aerodrome parking lot. FBI Agent Carol Toledo is with us. No one is at the abandoned house location. Tell the officers they need to approach cautiously."

"Will do. I'm sending out the call immediately."

"Thank you." Angie ended the call.

Morales lifted his remaining arm weakly. "Can I have my phone back?"

"No," Angie said. "But thanks for giving us the code. What was it again? Eleven-one-two?"

"Yes," Mee Mee said. "That's easy to remember."

"Why is that?" Carol asked.

"November first and second—The Day of the Dead."

# Chapter 34

Angie's favorite seafood restaurant in town was Rusty's Surf and Turf. Less than a mile from home, the place offered a variety of good food at reasonable prices. On a Thursday evening, a week after the successful rescue, they gathered there to celebrate. The seafoam-green one-story establishment welcomed locals and vacationers with a friendly atmosphere. Angie couldn't wait to sink her teeth into a juicy, medium-well-done ribeye steak.

As they mounted the steps to the front deck, Sammy asked Phoebe, "Do you need help carrying Midnight?"

"No. I can do it." Phoebe had clasped the cat around its belly, the feline's back legs almost touching the ground. When she reached the top step, Midnight meowed. She lowered the cat to the deck, and it rubbed its side against her legs.

"Remember," Joel said. "Midnight belongs to Carol."

"I know. I won't cry when we give him back to her."

They entered the establishment and spotted Mee Mee and Carol sitting at a large rectangular table in the rear. The pineapple yellow walls and amber tabletops brightened the interior, giving the place a cheerful ambiance. Seascapes from local artists graced the walls, and bluegrass music jangled in the background. Midnight took the lead, crossed the dining area and hopped up on the chair next to Carol.

"There's my beautiful spy." She reached and rubbed the cat's cheeks. Phoebe sat next to the cat, and Angie, Joel and Sammy took their seats on the other side of the rectangular table.

"I hope everybody is hungry," Mee Mee said. "The food here is spectacular."

"It sure smells good," Joel said. "I'm starved."

A blond wavy-haired waiter wearing jeans and a striped button-down shirt approached and said, "I'm sorry, but cats aren't allowed in the restaurant."

Carol straightened and eyed the man. "This is a service cat."

He tilted his head. "Really?"

Carol nodded.

"I didn't know there was a such thing as a service cat."

"Now you know," Carol said. "And since you are here, would you like to take our drink orders?"

"Sure thing." He snatched a pad and pen from his

back pocket to take their drink orders. Everybody opted for water except Phoebe. She wanted chocolate milk.

As he left the table Carol said, "Oh, and bring us a bottle of good white wine and wine glasses. We will be making some toasts."

The waiter stopped and about-faced. "Sure thing."

Mee Mee raised her hand. "Sorry, I don't drink. Bring me some apple or grape juice."

"Me, too," Sammy said. "I'm not twenty-one."

The waiter raised his hand and nodded. "Will do."

Carol shifted her focus to Joel. "Tell us about the drug raid, Detective Thomas."

Joel smiled. "Detective Thomas—I like the sound of that." He rubbed his hands together. "Well, with you ladies providing the combination to the gate and Morales's cellphone, you made our job a lot easier. We towed the Impreza and drove the pickup back to the blue house and parked them in the driveway. Then we set up camp there and began extracting information from his cellphone. El Mayo messaged Morales the next afternoon that they would be arriving about nine that night. We messaged them the gate code and replied: *Estaremos esperando tu llegada con los brazos abiertos.*

"We will be awaiting your arrival with open arms," Mee Mee interpreted.

Joel grinned. "And we were. When they entered the house, we arrested them without incident and confiscated a mother lode of cocaine and fentanyl."

"What kind of information did you get from the phone?" Carol asked.

"Lots of contacts and locations. Believe me. The DEA will be making a big dent in the drug and human trafficking trade on the east coast."

Mee Mee scooted up to the table. "What about Kiara's murderer? Any new leads there?"

"We arrested Diego Rivera. He spent almost a week in the hospital with a serious concussion."

Carol raised her hand. "I'll take credit for that."

"We believe he and his accomplice, José Garcia, killed Kiara. They made her ingest both mugwort and hemlock. After she succumbed to the poison, they dumped her body near the cabin to cast suspicion on Cora Mangas. Of course, Rivera blamed his dead friend. He'll be arraigned for murder later this week. His lawyer will probably want to work out a plea deal."

The waiter returned with their drinks and took their orders. Joel went with the Lemon Chicken, and Angie opted for the Kalbi, a grilled and marinated ribeye steak. Both Carol and Mee Mee ordered the Korean Style Mahi Mahi. Claiming she had gained a couple pounds recently, Sammy asked for the Greek Salad. Of course, Phoebe wanted her usual, a grilled cheese sandwich and fries.

When the waiter left their table, Carol sat back in her chair and said, "I have an important announcement to make."

Everyone quieted and turned toward her.

"Midnight has faithfully served his country now for six years. In a cat's life that is almost thirty years. Tonight, not only are we celebrating Joel's promotion and Sammy's rescue, but also Midnight's retirement. There's just one problem. We need to find him a good home."

Phoebe's eyes grew wide. "He can live with me!"

"Are you sure?"

Her head bobbed vigorously.

"We better ask your Mommy and Daddy."

"Why not?" Angie said. "He's been following me around for the last three weeks anyway. Let's make it permanent!"

"Fine with me," Joel said. "He's a good mouser."

Phoebe gathered the cat onto her lap and kissed its nose. "Now you're all mine." Midnight licked her chin.

For the next thirty minutes they talked, laughed and enjoyed their meals. After finishing her steak, Angie took out her cellphone and asked the blond waiter to take a picture of the crew.  They crowded together on one side of the table, and Phoebe cradled Midnight. The waiter snapped several photographs from different angles. They returned to their seats and passed the phone around to look at the photographs.

When Joel handed Angie back her phone, she couldn't help smiling. *We're all blessed to be alive.* She closed her eyes, and images of the last few weeks appeared and faded in her mind: confronting the teenagers at the Cora Tree, meeting Cora Mangas, the drug exchange at the Cape Hatteras Lighthouse, trailing the two cartel thugs, finding Kiara's body, the cabin fire, the home invasion, meeting Carol Toledo and rescuing Sammy. *The mission seemed impossible, but somehow, we did it. God was watching over us.* She sent up a quick prayer of thanksgiving. Above the din of the busy restaurant, she sensed a voice saying: *Keep up the good fight.*

Carol picked up the bottle of white wine and removed the cork. "The time has come for toasts." She filled her glass and passed the bottle to Joel. He poured the wine into Angie's glass and his glass. Carol raised her goblet. Mee Mee and Sammy lifted their glasses of apple juice. Phoebe, watching the adults, lifted her cup of chocolate milk.

"To my new friends," Carol said. "In my years as an agent for the Federal Bureau of Investigation, I have never served with a more courageous team."

"Cheers!" they all chimed and sipped their drinks.

Sammy lifted her glass. "I want to make a toast to these ladies who saved my life." She swallowed and blinked back tears. "You are all incredible."

"Cheers!" they all chimed and sipped their drinks.

Angie raised her glass. "I want to make a toast to Sammy. She saved my life five years ago. Last week when Morales had me in a headlock, she did it again. I still owe you one, kid."

"Cheers!" they all chimed and sipped their drinks.

Joel lifted his goblet. "I'd like to make a toast to

Mee Mee Roberts. She *dis-armed* one of the Sinaloa cartel's most notorious drug lords. And I mean that literally."

They all laughed and chimed, "Cheers!"

"What's going on here," a gravely man's voice said.

Angie sniffed raunchy cigar smoke and turned to see Detective Claudio, hands on his hips and a stump of a stogie in his mouth.

"Good evening, Detective Claudio," Joel said. "We're celebrating."

"I can see that." He removed the cigar and blew out a jet of gray smoke. "I've heard the news. Let me congratulate you on solving the two murders."

"Thank you," Angie said. "We gave it our best."

He rubbed his nose. "Of course, if the FBI hadn't pulled me from the case, I would have had it solved in a day or two."

"By the way." Angie unfolded her hand toward Carol. "I would like to introduce you to the FBI agent who took your place. This is Carol Toledo."

Claudio eyed Carol and grumbled, "Nice to meet you." He took a step back. "You look familiar. Have we met before?"

"I don't think so," Carol said.

"Well . . ." He glanced around the table. "I admit you all did nice work."

The blond waiter approached him. "I'm sorry, sir, but state law prohibits smoking inside of a restaurant."

"Oh . . . yes. I forgot." He held out his hand, the butt of the cigar between his thumb and finger. "Take care of this for me, would you, boy?"

The waiter took a napkin from the table and placed it in the palm of his hand. "Thank you for complying with the rules." He grimaced as Claudio dropped the stub into the napkin.

"No problem," Claudio grunted. "The law is the law." As the waiter turned to go, Claudio said, "Wait a minute, boy."

The waiter froze and faced him. "Yes, sir."

"I want you to bring me the bill for this party's meals. I'm paying for it."

"You don't have to do that," Angie protested.

"Oh no. I'm a man of my word. We had a bet. You said the witch's remains would be found in the ashes of the cabin. I was sure she was hiding in the woods, watching her shack burn to the ground. The FBI investigators found her bones in the ashes and identified them." He shifted his gaze to Carol. "Right, Agent Toledo?"

She nodded. "That is correct, sir."

"I lost the bet. I'll pay for your meal."

Angie eyed Carol and mouthed: *Should I tell him?*

She shook her head and whispered, "Still classified."

The waiter crossed the dining area and stepped up to Claudio. "Here's the bill."

"Thank you." He glanced at the total, scrunched up his face, lowered the bill, angled his head to work out a kink in his neck and said, "You guys don't eat cheap, do you?"

Angie couldn't keep a grin from broadening her face. "Give me the bill, Detective Claudio. I'll pay for it."

"No, no, no. I've got it covered." He turned and waddled toward the cash register, mumbling to himself.

Mee Mee snickered, "Now that display of unbridled generosity made this meal even tastier."

Everyone laughed.

"Wait a minute," Joel said. "Mee Mee, you haven't given a toast yet."

Mee Mee raised her glass of apple juice. "I'd like to make a toast to Robert Thornhill."

Angie knotted her brow. "Who is Robert Thornhill?"

Mee Mee grinned. "Ten years ago, he taught me how to fly an airplane."

"Cheers!"

I hope you enjoyed *The Cora Tree Murder*. If you did, please post a rating and review on Amazon.com or BarnesandNoble.com.

If you would like to discover how Angie Stallone began her career in the private investigation business, please check out my previous Outer Banks detective series (Weston Wolf Outer Banks Detective Series). In this three-book series, Angie teams up with Detective Weston Wolf to solve a variety of cases full of twists and turns. Also check out *A Nags Head Murder – An Angie Stallone Detective Mystery*.

**Click on the links below to go to the Amazon Kindle page.**

# Weston Wolf Outer Banks Detective Series

These are stand-alone novels and can be read in any order.

**The Roanoke Island Murders: A Modern Retelling of the Maltese Falcon**

**The Singer in the Sound: A Weston Wolf OBX Detective Novel**

**Kitty Hawk Confidential: A Weston Wolf OBX Detective Novel**

**Weston Wolf Outer Banks Detective – Three Book Set**

You may be interested in my first Outer Banks series. If you enjoy the Outer Banks and reading murder mysteries, please check them out.

# Outer Banks Murder Series

These are stand-alone novels and can be read in any order.

The Healing Place (Prequel to Murder at Whalehead)

Book 1 – Murder at Whalehead

Book 2 – Murder at Hatteras

Book 3 – Murder on the Outer Banks

Book 4 – Murder at Ocracoke

Book 5 – The Treasure of Portstmouth Island

Outer Banks Murder Series 5-Book Set

**Other books by Joe C. Ellis**

**A Nags Head Murder**

**The First Shall Be Last: A Novel of Love and War**

**The Old Man and the Marathon**

## About the Author

Joe C. Ellis, a big fan the North Carolina's Outer Banks, grew up in the Ohio Valley. A native of Martins Ferry, Ohio, he attended West Liberty State College in West Virginia and went on to earn his master's degree in education from Muskingum College in New Concord, Ohio. After a thirty-six-year career as an art teacher, he retired from the Martins Ferry City School District.

Currently, he is the pastor for the Scotch Ridge Presbyterian Church and the Colerain Presbyterian Church. His writing career began in 2001 with the publication of his first novel, *The Healing Place*. In 2007 he began the *Outer Banks Murder Series* with the publication of *Murder at Whalehead* (2010), *Murder at Hatteras* (2011), *Murder on the Outer Banks* (2012), *Murder at Ocracoke* (2017), and The *Treasure of Portsmouth Island* (2019).

Most recently Joe has completed the Outer Banks Detective Series which includes three books: Roanoke Island Murders (2020), The Singer in the Sound (2021), Kitty Hawk Confidential (2021), and A Nags Head Murder (2023).

Joe credits family vacations on the Outer Banks with the

inspiration for his stories. Joe and his wife Judy have three children and nine grandchildren.  Although the kids have flown the nest, they get together often and always make it a priority to vacation on the Outer Banks whenever possible. He comments, "It's a place on the edge of the world, a place of great beauty and sometimes danger — the ideal setting for murder mysteries."